TAKe A
look FAC... GAiL →

© 2002 Steven Gibbs
Published by Benoy Publishing
735 H Bragg Drive
Wilmington, North Carolina 28412

ISBN 0-9720809-2-9
LCCN 2002106133

Printed in the United States

Lazarus
Milkshake

*"From each, according to his ability;
to each, according to his need."*—**Karl Marx**

This book is dedicated to the most beautiful Sky.
You have given me more than you will ever know.

Foreword

The following stories play for us a moving picture of an otherwise still life world. Steven places among us a prism of imagination by wondering beyond the look in a stranger's eyes. His stories are stolen glimpses into their curious existence. Individually, intriguing characters expose the freedom, folly, and fate of the masses. Some are trying to escape and others, in their own way, attempt to transcend. All sense a predetermination. Ultimately, their routes have been chosen already.

Jack Crosby is marked from the beginning, crippled by a freak accident and bound to a life of poor chance. *Hal Patterson* is the politician who says what we want to hear AND does what he says (positively good fiction!). Hal consciously creates change but falls short in controlling his own destiny.

Some characters live for the day and others can make a moment last a feature length film. Throughout the compilation there is a twinkle of self-reliance and we see individual choice splashing about in the stream of what is meant to be, **"the constant battle of blood and veins"**. Emerson says it this way: *"Our faith comes in moments; our vice is habitual. Yet there is a depth in those brief moments which constrains us to ascribe more reality to them than all other experiences."* Steven reveals both our desire to disappear and our will to squeeze a little more than life has planned. Based on his own experiences of peripheral existence and wacky escapades, he can convincingly tell the tale of those on the fringe. He and his bag of fiction are bound for greatness...as I knew they always would be.

Tiana Viveralli: *Morne Trois Pitons, Dominica, W.I.*

TABLE OF CONTENTS

Pellagra

"When I was young I used to wait, on master and hand him his plate. Pass him the bottle when he got dry, and brush away the blue-tail fly. Jimmy crack corn, and I don't care...My master's gone away." - **Traditional Folk Song**

1

Heavy rain covers the city. Worms scatter themselves across the concrete sidewalk. Darryl tries unsuccessfully to step around each one. The rain feels cold against his face. Darryl counts three worms stepped on for every block he travels. He estimates a total of eighteen to twenty worms will perish before he can walk safely across the dry green floor of the cafeteria. It is early morning, he makes short, non-denominational prayers for each worm.

The door of the school opens easily. The hallway is empty and shadowed with a glow of fluorescent lights. Darryl can hear the conversation from the kitchen staff. He tucks in his shirt as he walks. He checks his appearance in an office window before he opens the kitchen door. He examines the rash developing on his neck.

"Hey, it's Mr. Corn."

"Morning, Kernel."

Darryl smiles with acknowledgement at his co-workers. He enters a small office and places his coat on a hook behind the door. He studies the afternoon menu. The schedule has become complex since the contest. Bread pudding for dessert and a choice of fried chicken or plain spaghetti as an entré. There is also corn bread and corn salad.

Darryl forgets the worms on the sidewalk. He looks out his office door. One of the dishwashers waves to him with both hands. Darryl returns the gesture, then closes the door and sits down in his chair. He examines the award on his desk. It is a wooden plaque with his name engraved on a small piece of metal. There is a brass corncob positioned in the center with the number one above it. Darryl looks closely at the number. The honor seems strange to him now.

2

"How are you today, Darryl?"

"I'm fine. How are things this morning?"

"Just another day."

"Has anyone started cutting bread for the pudding?"

"We're using the bread from yesterday."

"Pork sandwich."

"Yes."

"Ok, let me put my apron on and I'll join you."

"The exchange student has been asking about you."

"Since the contest?"

"That's not the reason."

Darryl makes direct eye contact with the woman as she speaks. He notices a twitch in her left eye. He assumes it is a signal of misconception and he ignores the remainder of the conversation. Darryl ties the apron tight around his large waist and pulls a pair of latex gloves onto his hands. He enjoys the clean and sanitary feeling of the gloves.

Darryl is quiet this morning. The employees have overwhelmed him since he returned from Millersport last month. He has made it obvious that the attention is beginning to disturb him.

Darryl is overweight. His legs are thick and he becomes tired after walking long distances. His face is scarred from acne. He wears contact lenses and rarely bathes himself. His body odor is minimal. Darryl was born with weak sweat glands.

"Hey, Kernel, what type of sauce should I open? Meat or plain tomato?"

"Plain."

"Looks like we might run out."

"We'll use the meat if we have to."

Darryl has thinning brown hair that he keeps tied behind his back in a short braided ponytail. He stands awkwardly at the stainless steel table. His legs are slightly bent to distribute his weight properly. He has become comfortable with his size and has trained himself to remain slightly active. He walks a short distance each day after work and occasionally swims in his neighbor's pool. A woman approaches Darryl; she is tall and wears a blue hairnet.

"Are these carrots still good?"

"Just soak them in water. They should be fine."

"Thank you, Mr. Corn."

Darryl releases a genuine laugh and returns to his work. He slices the bread into uniform squares for the pudding. He scratches the back of his neck with a paper towel.

3

The Sweet Corn Festival is held once a year in Millersport on the weekend before Labor Day. The town is twenty-five miles East of Columbus. The fairgrounds were donated to the city by the Millersport chapter of the Lions

Club. The festival is a non-profit organization to fund local and national charities. The weekend is complete with a midway, live entertainment, and a corn-eating competition.

Darryl's brother convinced him to attend the event. He told Darryl it was a great place to meet single women in the area. Darryl has never been married and he seldom attends any social functions. He enjoys horror films and collects antique cooking utensils.

Darryl and his brother are identical twins. They were born at Riverside Hospital in the Northern section of Columbus. Darryl's grandfather owns a gas station near the main highway. Darryl and his brother worked there during high school. The money helped Darryl attend two semesters at Capital College. Darryl is now the cafeteria supervisor at Cranbrook Elementary in Columbus. His managerial skills in the kitchen have brought the school a much-needed improvement to the quality of food service.

4

Darryl opens a container of egg whites; he delicately adds the mixture to a pan of milk and cut bread. It is Thursday and the kitchen is busy. Darryl begins to open large boxes of frozen chicken. The morning hours pass slowly.

The school has introduced a new policy for safe food handling. Cafeteria employees are required to wash their hands once every half hour. A logbook near the sink must be filled out and signed after each wash. Darryl believes the system invades personal rights and creates conflict with time management. He signs his name sixteen times each morning. He wears latex gloves.

Darryl stands behind empty boxes of chicken. A young woman approaches him. He smiles and continues his work.

"The noodles are ready to make and I opened the green beans."

"You can help me with the chicken."

"What about corn?"

"We'll do that last."

The young woman is an exchange student from the university. She is required by her sponsor to work two mornings each week during her visit. She is a thin, assertive woman from Japan. Her hair is a deep black, partially revealed under a hairnet. She wears a t-shirt from the Rotary Club. Darryl watches her closely as she pulls the chicken from its package. Her arms are a perfect bronze, which blend terrifically with the dark color of her eyes. She amuses herself as the chicken parts are pulled from their package and placed under running water.

"You were in a dream of mine last night."

Darryl reaches for a sheet pan as the girl speaks. He places the pan on the table and begins to position the chicken in even layers. He says nothing to the girl. Darryl offers her a pan and she attempts to simulate his methods of chicken placement.

"It was a strange dream, things moving very fast and we were working in the kitchen."

"Dreams can be strange sometimes."

"You were cooking sausage and I was playing with children toys."

The conversation becomes uncomfortable for Darryl. He scratches at the rash on his neck. He fills another pan with chicken parts. The young girl asks for a pair of latex gloves. Darryl explains how to put them on properly and how to avoid tearing the rubber. They work together silently, placing frozen chicken parts on metal pans.

5

At the Corn Festival, Darryl's brother managed to point and stare at any suitable woman. He told Darryl stories about past relationships. Darryl kept quiet. He was amazed at the dedication the town shared in the cultivation of corncobs. They paused briefly near the main stage to watch a children's musical performance. The concession booths were stocked with local varieties of sweet corn. The fairgrounds were crowded. The brothers sampled some of the region's most prestigious corn. They are comparable in size. Darryl is slightly larger and displays a more reserved personality.

Darryl's lack of communication skills provided little entrance into conversations with possible females. The twins experimented with the midway and the craft booths. Simple comments on their identical appearances were all they received.

Near the main tent, Darryl's brother noticed a large yellow sign promoting the corn-eating competition. The brothers determined that the situation could create an honest exchange of dialog with single women. It was common ground. The eating contest was their method of romanticism.

6

The exchange student sings as she applies a layer of vegetable base to the pans. Darryl watches her closely. He admires her grace and the firm structure of her facial bones. The girl's name is Mari. She wears a distracting perfume and a bright lip-gloss covers her mouth.

Darryl finishes preparing the last box of chicken. He looks over the menu

4

again and exhales loudly. The girl offers her assistance with the corn salad. She is persistent. Darryl instructs her to open two cases of frozen corn kernel and a large container of diced tomatoes. The kitchen staff begins to watch the interaction of Mari and Darryl.

"Put the bags of corn under cold water."

"Not hot?"

"I need the tomatoes in a large stock pot."

"Ok."

Mari carefully opens the boxes of corn, placing each bag perfectly in the sink. She rinses her gloves with the running water before pouring the tomatoes. She moves around the kitchen with elegance. Her legs bend gracefully as she approaches Darryl. She looks around the kitchen.

"I see corn trophy in the office, the girls tell me you won it in the contest."

"It's not a big deal."

"A trophy is."

"All I did was eat."

"You were fastest."

"And now the principal wants a corn dish on every lunch menu. It's ridiculous."

"It is a symbol."

"I suppose."

"People like symbols, it is something to honor."

"It's not what I expected."

"What did you expect?"

Darryl stretches his back and repositions his feet. He scratches at the rash. He motions his shoulders at her question. He thinks again about the worms struggling against the rubber bottoms of shoes.

7

Darryl and his brother entered themselves into the first heat of the contest. One ear of corn was timed during consumption. Darryl advanced into the second heat and managed to win by three seconds. His talent was recognized immediately. Darryl's brother lost the first challenge. He attempted to impress a young woman in the audience.

Darryl was invited back the next day to challenge the other heat winners in the grand championship of the Millersport Sweet Corn Festival. Darryl was persuaded to stay an extra day by one of the judges who appeared to have an interest in his abilities. His brother paid for a hotel room. The two stayed up late drinking beer and talking about their female aspirations.

8

Darryl did not anticipate the recognition that *Sweet Corn Grand Champion* would bring. Immediately following the event, Darryl was photographed for the *Columbus Dispatch* and given a lengthy interview. His brother was proud. Darryl was nervous. He did not sweat or show enthusiasm.

The Lions Club honored Darryl with a small award and a wreath of Indian Corn. His name was announced over the speaker system each hour. Darryl became a celebrity. Two young women offered him their phone numbers and managed to fondle his braided hair. His personality attempted to handle the increase of self-esteem.

The following day his photograph was published on the first page in the local section of the newspaper. Relatives and neighbors began to telephone Darryl throughout the day. His co-workers had a party for him. His job performance suffered and he began to lose sleep. He soon developed a rash on his elbow, which has recently spread to his neck.

9

Mari begins to question Darryl about his success in the competition. Her English is easily understood. Darryl carries the stockpot to the stove.

"In Japan, it is a tradition to believe everyone is responsible for their own actions. The results of each action is in relation to the previous action."

"That sounds reasonable."

"It is not sin to be good at things."

"I'm aware of that, Mari."

"And what do you think?"

"This is about corn."

"The symbol is something else."

"I don't want to become an icon."

"What is it you want?"

"I want these tomatoes to simmer."

"You did bring the trophy to work."

Darryl pauses and examines the brass corncob from across the room. The number one stands proudly above the corn. He sees an employee wash her hands, then sign the list above the sink. He turns toward the stove, mixing the tomatoes slowly around the pot. Mari hands Darryl a package of corn and a container of chopped green peppers.

"This salad you are cooking, is it in completion?"

"I don't think so."

"In your head it is complete, but it takes many pieces to make one whole."

"What?"

"Physical pieces."

"Incompletion?"

"Similar to Mr. Corn."

"How?"

"Mr. Corn is only part of you, it is not you entirely."

"So, I'm incomplete?"

"You cannot have a whole without little pieces."

"What if you have no little pieces?"

"Pieces are everywhere. You have to pull them together."

Darryl notices the kitchen staff watching the progression of their dialogue. He continues to stir the tomatoes as he adds the corn and green peppers to the stockpot. Mari opens the remaining bags of corn. The latex provides excellent grip.

10

Mari is aware of the rash on Darryl's neck. He has been to three doctor's appointments since the contest. The spread of the rash is discomforting to the entire staff. The doctor claims it is not contagious. Darryl has seen it increase in size over the past three weeks.

"Have the doctors said new things about your problem?"

"They don't know anything."

"It does not look so bad."

"Maybe my actions created it."

"Possible."

"My brother assumes it's from a lack of vitamins. I think it might be from the chlorine in my neighbor's pool."

11

Following the triumph in Millersport, Darryl was approached by various farms from around the region. Publicity agents photographed Darryl with the farm owners. He was offered several cases of corn to sample and was asked to give written opinions on each variety.

Shortly after Darryl arrived back in Columbus, he received sixty pounds of corncob. He was asked by the *Ohio Corn Growers Association* to appear in a series of magazine advertisements. Darryl declined the proposal and was given a certified *OCGA* sweatshirt and duffel bag for his accomplishment in the festival.

"I get tired of corn."

"Principal likes it on the menu."

"With all the corn I have in my freezer, I've made every dish possible."

Mari adds bags of corn to the stockpot as Darryl stirs. The two begin to speak loudly as the spatula scrapes the inside of the pot. Their conversation is heard by the kitchen staff. Darryl adjusts the temperature and adds a mixture of salt and pepper to the corn salad. He tells Mari to continue stirring as he returns to the chair in his office. He removes the latex gloves and examines his neck in a small mirror set on the desk. The telephone rings.

"Darryl?"

"Yes."

"I think I found the vitamin deficiency behind your rash."

"How?"

"I've been in the reference section all morning."

"At the library?"

"Who else has a reference section?"

"I don't know."

"Listen to this."

"Why are you so interested in my health?"

"What else do I have to do? And now I feel partially responsible."

"How are you responsible?"

"Just listen. It says here that the rash might be a symptom of another disease."

"Are you calling me from the library?"

"From a pay phone in the hallway.'

"Ok."

"The symptoms you have resemble a disease that relates to a lack of niacin."

"Niacin?"

"It says that a lack of niacin can cause the symptoms."

"Cause what symptoms?"

"Your disease."

"Disease? It's a rash from the chlorine."

"A nutritionist states that corn has very small amounts of niacin, almost none at all."

"What is it?"

"I guess it's an important supplement."

"I'm in the middle of something right now."

"Let me read you this paragraph about the psychological effects."

"I'm talking to a woman."

"The Korean one?"

"She's from Japan."

"Just listen."

"Call me after lunch, I need to start the cornbread."

"That's what I'm telling you, it's the corn."

Darryl places the telephone down. He examines his neck once more, then returns to the kitchen. Mari has removed the corn salad from the stove and is placing it in aluminum containers. Darryl locates a fresh pair of gloves and opens a large bag of cornbread mix. He pours half of the bag into a round bowl. Mari finishes covering the corn salad with plastic wrap.

Darryl instructs a young man to warm the spaghetti sauce. He articulates the sentence with a sudden authority. Mari walks toward Darryl. Her mouth opens wide as she speaks. Her lip-gloss has begun to fade.

"We are near finished. We have to refresh milk and juices."

"Someone needs to set the fruit too."

"I think it is done already."

"Do you want to help me with this bread?"

"Yes."

"If we take our break early, maybe we can talk more."

"Sure."

"And maybe go somewhere a different time, not around work?"

Darryl holds his breath for a moment. He becomes confused and light-headed. He looks out the window at the rain. His thoughts become disordered. He remembers the dying worms and the corn wreath on his bedroom wall. He changes the placement of his feet on the kitchen floor. Mari is embarrassed by the silence. She steps away from the table and removes her gloves. She washes her hands in the sink and signs her name on the required list.

Darryl collects his thoughts. He does not sweat or become visibly nervous. He watches Mari as she replaces the list on the wall. He smiles and scratches his neck.

"Maybe we could go swimming sometime."

"I thought that is how you got the rash."

"My brother might be right about the vitamins."

"And if he is not?"

"The actions will create the result."

"Yes."

"Tomorrow?"

"If it stops raining."

"The pool is heated too."

"I'll call you when my classes are over."

"Ok."

Darryl passes his tongue along his upper lip as he reads the directions on the cornbread package. He places a wet towel around his neck to calm the agitation of the rash. He does not sweat. Darryl looks toward his office door.

The award leans perfectly against the wall. The number one shines under the light of a desk lamp. His name is engraved deep into the plaque. For a moment, Darryl is proud. He looks around with an arrogant grin as the worms continue to perish and the rash continues to spread.

Dog Gone

"Go forth, light and heavy; and strive with yourselves and your wealth in the path of Allah. That is better for you, if you only knew." - **Qurán, 9:41**

1

The morning air lingers with the familiar scent of cat urine and gasoline. Water Street resonates with the sound of faint human voices and the weary engines of automobiles. The sun has taken its place on the horizon. The pigeons are silent. Dust fills my nostrils as I reach for my sunglasses. An empty container of milk sits paralyzed on an apartment doorstep. A city bus begins its daily rituals. This is big city Wisconsin.

Walter rides his bicycle down the sidewalk. I can see him from a distance as I walk. He seems content with his surroundings. The clouds paint pictures of lollipops and beauty salons as they cast shadows on the asphalt. Milwaukee has never looked so beautiful.

Walter rides in continuous circles at the intersection. He wears an aged pair of army surplus binoculars around his neck and his hair shifts in the wind while he sings to himself. The black vinyl pouch on his handle bars is flopping in rhythm to his circular motions.

This is our tenth month of business together. Walter has been a faithful partner and a man of extreme detail. Each building we pass, he delicately scans the alley and fire escapes for traces of present or past canine activity. Tuesday afternoon he spotted a pregnant Llapso Apso living behind a men's shoe store. She was worth an easy fifty dollars. Business has been good. Each morning the lost and found section of the classifieds seems to grow with possibilities. Our financial situation is on the rise.

It's my job to return the dogs to the owner, since Walter's social skills are clearly nonexistent. He said from the start he would have nothing to do with locating cats. He rationalized that he is in this for Nessie and since cats are known to eat fish, they can stay lost and unfound for all he cares. He also believes that the entertainment community is in control of everything we do and say. He believes actors and actresses work for the government to inhibit population growth. Walter contends that drug abuse and suicide have tripled since the invention of television and motion pictures.

I approach the intersection and can clearly make out Walter's song. He is singing the first few lines of *Git Along Little Dogies*, a traditional cowboy folk song that appears to have become his personal hymn for the past six weeks. I immediately join in the next verse:

"It's early in the spring that we round up the dogies, And mark 'em and brand 'em and cut off their tails. We round up our horses and load on the chuck wagon, And throw the dogies out onto the trail."

"Morning Leo."

"How you doing Walter."

"I think I saw that Shepherd mix from the other day."

Walter stands up, his bike is motionless as he balances, one foot on the left pedal and one on the ground. He wears a red flannel shirt and cut-off jean shorts. This is the fourth time in two days he has mentioned the Shepherd mix. His mustache disguises his lips as he speaks. I have concluded his mental state to be partly schizophrenic with a slight blend of anxiety and frequent mood swings. He has never been professionally diagnosed that I know of.

When I was seventeen my mother took me to see a psychologist. His office was on the west side between a clothing store and an eye glass repair center. The walls of his office were decorated with various paintings of children carrying balloons. One scene showed a young girl with two balloons. One balloon was floating in the air, the other was deflated near her feet. I told the doctor that he should paint over the balloon on the ground. He wrote my suggestion on a sheet of yellow notebook paper and offered me a piece of hard candy.

2

Walter and I meet five days a week at sunrise. I bring the classifieds from the day before and we begin our search. We sometimes cover fifty miles in one day. We average two or three dogs a week, collecting about seventy-five dollars for each of us per week.

There's an ad in the paper this morning for a Golden Retriever. He is said to be wearing a green collar and answers to the name *Lumpy*. A reward is mentioned. I call the telephone number and no one answers. Walter mentions the Shepherd mix again. I hop on the seat of his bike and Walter pedals down the street. The bicycle is a 1978 blue ten-speed from a Sears Department Store. He has kept up on its basic maintenance although the chain falls off quite often and the gears are severely in need of oiling.

He told me he found the bike five years ago behind a bar near the beach when he was searching for partial beers in the dumpster. He introduced this technique of street life to me on our first day together. Since then we usually conclude each day's work with the bar alley beverages. Swallowing warm alcohol and the occasional wet cigarette reminds me of the complexities of

God and what sort of life he has given me. I sometimes feel selfish to want more. The Creator has given us this life and a beautiful place to perform in it. We have destroyed it. We have become our own enemy. Walter tells me he feels sympathetic for the flowers and weeds that try to squeeze through the cracks in the sidewalk. He calls the situation a semi-vicious social blanket. I'm not sure why.

3

I stole a book last summer from the public library titled *In Search of Mohammed*. It had a photograph of an enormous city with a computer enhanced rainbow on the cover along with the fist of a dark skinned male. I thought it was a book about boxing and the legendary Cassius Clay. I was then fighting on the street to earn extra money aside from the monotonous can recycling. My boxing career was slowly diminishing and I needed advice. I was losing sixty percent of the money I put down on myself.

After reading the first three chapters, I discovered the words and paragraphs inside were not about boxing, but about the Muslim religion and the holy significance of the Saudi Arabian city, Mecca.

The Muslim faith employs a relatively large amount of followers, second only to Christianity. They believe that around 600 AD a man named Mohammed was the last great prophet and that God goes by the name Allah. Mohammed declared Mecca a holy city and wrote Allah's direct words in a story known as the Qurán. Like Christianity, the religion is divided into separate sects and demoninations but its believers mostly adhere to five basic principles: faith in Allah as the only God, praying to the creator five times a day, charity work, fasting for the Ramadan holiday, and to make a pilgrimage to Mecca at least once in your lifetime on planet earth.

A one way plane ticket from Milwaukee to the Mecca area is $1,229.00. A costly procedure for religious sanctity. I have saved a little more than nine hundred dollars. These dogs are constructing my tower in the sky.

Only a true member of the Islamic faith can gain entrance into the holy city. This makes it even more desirable. I'll have to use my instinct and creative knowledge to gain access to their pearled gates. They can't keep the holy kingdom under lock and key. It's all in how you present yourself Walter says.

All we have here is a few famous breweries and a polluted coastline. Wisconsin is not very fulfilling. I figure if I make it to Mecca and can't find God or a reasonable facsimile, there should at least be some fine young women looking for a good time with an intelligent self employed man from

13

the United States. The way things are going here, a pilgrimage can only be a good thing.

4

A mile or two into our journey, Walter's bike chain disconnects and we stop at the corner of Juneau and Water Street. There is a slight wind and the sun is now fully visible between clouds. I step off the bicycle, my pants covered in grease from the chain. As Walter refastens our transportation, I scan the classifieds. A reward is offered for a Siberian Husky that was lost in the same area we now occupy.

Walter mumbles something about the Shepherd mix as I question random people about the Husky. This is the way we work. Walter walks and I talk. A group of young boys tell me they saw the dog yesterday at the park around the corner. Walter and I assemble the bike and pedal down to the scene.

5

Walter spends most of his nights sleeping in an abandoned motel on the North side where he keeps his few belongings including his goldfish, Nessie. He keeps her in an orange plastic container near the windowsill in one of the upstairs rooms. About a week before I met Walter, Nessie came down with dropsy, a rare disease produced by a bacterial infection causing internal bleeding which leads to a swollen abdomen, destroying the internal organs. He takes her to a veterinarian twice a week to be bathed in a solution of Maracyn-Two and Tetracyline. The procedure is rather inexpensive but Walter's obsessive and frequent visits keep him working hard. After the news of Nessie's illness became an issue, Walter immediately doubled his aluminum recycling efforts and began an illegal paper route.

He would pay for one newspaper from a vending machine and take the entire bundle. He would then resell the paper below cost at different areas in town. Around this same time, I had returned my first dog to its owner and received my first reward. I began searching newspapers and telephone poles for more lost animals when I came across Walter on the street and convinced him to sell me a classified section for ten cents. He agreed, while our lucrative business ideas and similar life conditions led us into a conversation about a dog he had seen earlier that day, a Shepherd mix.

We began our pursuit and haven't stopped yet. We are good at what we do. Last week, channel 58 did a story on us: *The Homeless Heroes*. We didn't talk much in front of the camera and the reporter's awkward voice patterns made both of us nervous. The station bought us lunch and gave us each thirty dollars.

6

We arrive at the park and lean the bicycle against the stairs of a slide. Walter claims the slide would be worth a lot at the recycling center. He even comes up with a plan on how to get it there. I ignore his speech and walk over to the swing set.

"Hey Leo, over here by the castle."

"What?"

"There's a few dog prints in the sand and some fresh piss on the support beams."

It's situations like this when I'm glad I never went to college. Money is easy. Walter makes a few well thought out whistles and barks as I scan the surroundings. I see no dog in sight. There is a small wooded area behind the park that Walter walks through, patting each blade of grass with his sneakers. He surveys the playground with his binoculars as he sings:

"Whoopee ti yi yo, git along little dogies, It's your misfortune and none of my own. Whoopee ti yi yo, git along little dogies, for you know Wyoming will be your new home."

We return to the bike and head downtown. Along the way, Walter explains his opinion on my pilgrimage. The bike chain stays attached the entire ride.

"You know Leo, this Mecca place, you think it's safe, with all that war and oil stuff?"

"They say it's a holy city."

"Yeah I know that, but what about the women in veils and the Samurais and the nuclear bomb testing and all the religious wars."

"I think you looked at too many of those newspapers you were selling."

"There wasn't much else to do."

"That's why I'm trying to get there."

We stop at a pay phone on Third Street and I call the Golden Retriever ad again. The woman who answers gives me a better description and tells us the reward is one hundred fifty dollars. It is pure bred, ready for mating, and possibly stolen from her backyard. She says she had seen us on the news and hoped we would call. I told her we'd call her back if anything was found. She said good luck and told me to tell Walter hello.

7

Walter and I eat breakfast from a convenience store. Walter has two chocolate donuts. I ingest a grapefruit and a corn muffin. I have given up meat in hope of a better reception in the holy land. Walter transports us to the section of town where the Retriever was last seen. The chain links are doing well today. We stop in every alley and ask every fifth person we see. This is a system of mathematics and averages that Walter conceived since day one. It's all about probability he says.

Two hours later we stop for coffee at a small diner. After we sit down, Walter smiles at me and jumps out of his seat, nervously fondling a woman with his plastic spoon. I grab him and quickly apologize for his behavior as we rush out the door, spilling coffee all around us. Walter hops on the bicycle and pedals away. This is not the first time I have seen one of his episodes. He explained to me that they are often caused by false scenery on wallpaper. This particular occurrence was due to a repetitive pattern of wheat fields around the diner's corridor.

I walk the next few blocks alone, scanning the alleys and store fronts. It has been a slow morning. We rarely deal with the city's animal control or Humane Societies. The profit loss is too large. We give a dog two or three days and move on. A man walking ahead of me enters a bank and throws a lit cigarette on the concrete. I grab it and pull it to my lips. I can see Walter in the background. His head is turning in circles:

"As I was a walking one morning for pleasure, I spied a cowpuncher a riding along. His hat was throwed back and his spurs were a jingling. As he approached me singing this song."

8

I can hear the squeak of his axles and see that he holds something small in his hand. When he arrives next to me he says nothing, handing me a green dog collar with a steel tag that reads: *Lumpy.*

Walter's gums bleed due to lack of brushing. I can see the build up of plaque on his bottom teeth. He tells me he saw the Retriever three blocks from where we stand. He tried to grab him but the collar came loose and the dog got away. He examines some of *Lumpy's* hair follicles that are stuck in his fingernails. He continues to explain the situation with an endless supply of details and discomfort. There is a dandelion sprouting near his feet. Walter stops his story in mid sentence.

"*Lumpy.* Come here boy."

"Is that him, Walter?"

"Sure is. He's a beauty ain't he."

"Get the leash ready."

The Retriever walks with a slight limp. He has forgotten about Walter. I grab a dog biscuit from the pouch on Walter's bike. I call *Lumpy* to my side. Walter slips the collar on him, tightly fastens our makeshift leash, and we walk *Lumpy* to the nearest pay phone.

Within the hour we each have another seventy-five dollars and are busy searching the lost and found section. I am five dogs from Mecca.

"What about this Pomeranian, Leo?"

"I think we should go for the Border Collie. I can tell by the wording that the owner has a lot of money."

"Just cause they say: Greatly missed?"

"No, because they say: *Valued family dog with a friendly glow.*"

We both agree, and after a lengthy phone conversation with the owner, we ride off in the direction of the dog's recent departure. The bike chain comes off three times before we arrive in Glendale, a middle class section of the city. Walter is sweating profanely and asks me where the Shepherd mix is while he stares into the reflection of the sun on passing cars. I ignore his behavior as I scan our environment. I see nothing but roof tops and basketball hoops. The neighborhood is empty. Two birds rest on a telephone wire. I can hear a lawn mower dancing in the background. We quickly head back to town.

9

Nessie lies with her stomach facing the ceiling as her camouflaged body floats continuously around the orange container. Her eyes have turned pale and her gills are dormant. Her fins and scales are protruding. She is twice her normal size. The dropsy has gotten her. Walter had more than enough money to put her through fifteen more treatments and was hoping to surprise her by buying a ten gallon aquarium with colored gravel and plastic seaweed. He stands patiently over the fish bowl:

"Your mother she was raised a-way down in Texas, Where the Jimson weed and sandburs grow. Now we'll fill you up on prickly pear and cholla, Till you are ready for the trail to Idaho."

Walter picks Nessie up by her tail. Her appearance is lively in his shaking hands. He takes a small piece of aluminum foil and wraps her inside it. He puts the fish in his hand and walks to the other side of the room. I hear him say something about Milwaukee as he digs through a pile of newspapers on the floor. He turns toward me, his flannel shirt unbuttoned, revealing his mis-shaped nipples and his self-inflicted tattoos.

"I want you to take Nessie with you."

"Take her where?"

"Arabia, and bury her in the ground. She deserves it. Here's three hundred dollars. Buy the ticket and leave this place."

"I can't take your money, Walter."

17

"I have more. And besides, you have to. For Nessie. I think God might want it this way. I'm quitting the business anyway. My legs are tired. I need a vacation. Take the money. Take her. There's not much else to do. That's why you're going, right?"

10

Mrs. Landon remembers my face when I enter the office. It is my third visit this week. She looks frustrated and says nothing. I sit down in front of the desk and flash my passport. She sips her coffee and breathes heavily through her nose.

"Can I help you Leo?"

I hand her $1,229.00. Her face is puzzled. Ninety-seven dollars of it is in quarters. She counts the change and whistles a song. She knows what I want. I have continually checked air fare rates for the past eleven weeks. I was vaccinated for Meningitis and received my visa three months ago. She turns to her computer and quickly types a few lines. She takes my passport from the desk to make a photocopy of it. She returns to her seat, smiling at me while the computer prints out my ticket.

It's women like Mrs. Landon that make life in the United States so intolerable. It's an indescribable personality trait that seems to be a part of most citizens. Walter calls this mannerism Cold-Love. He sees it all over town, especially in grocery stores and public rest rooms.

Nessie's aluminum coffin rests in my pocket. I leave the travel agency and walk to Elder's Cafe. I have enough money to buy a nice meal and a newspaper. My plane leaves in three days. I will eventually land in Riyadh, then travel by bus to Mecca.

I reread my ticket constantly. Milwaukee is my past. Salvation is my future. The domestication of animals has blessed me with a path of right-eousness. The death of a goldfish has given me the monetary provisions to complete my spiritual crusade. I read the world news. There was a small plane crash in Pakistan. A man was arrested for multiple bank robbery in Australia.

11

I meet Walter at 10:30 behind the arrangement of bars on Brady Street. The moon is nearly full and Walter appears to be functioning well. He asks me to see Nessie again. I pass him the foil wrapper. He holds it tight in his hand for a moment, reminding me to bury her deep. I return the fish to my pocket as Walter hands me a bottle of beer with the label partially torn off. There are a few sips left. We toast to Nessie and to my future in Saudi Arabia. Walter has bought a new chain for his bike. He wears a bracelet made from the old chain. I encourage him to continue the business, but he declines, citing the unnecessary benefits of it all.

"I want to show you something, Leo."

"What is it?"

"Wyoming."

"The state?"

Walter laughs and then calls out, "Wyoming, Wyoming, Here girl."

A short brown dog runs around the corner. I can see shadows of dripping saliva as it comes toward us. She wears a red bandanna around her neck and has a tail the size of her body length. Walter says Wyoming is part German Shepherd. He thinks she might have some Pincher in her. He found her in the front of his motel and she followed him all the way here.

Walter believes she has been looking for him for the past six months and the constant distraction of our business has delayed their meeting.

I offer the dog a sip of my beer as Walter pillages through the dumpster, pulling out meat scraps for Wyoming. I look at my plane ticket as Walter feeds his new friend. The glare of the street light helps me read it aloud. Walter brushes the hair out of his eyes, and pats Wyoming on her head. A light turns on. Voices come from one of the backdoors. Walter sets down his beer and jumps on to his bike seat. He wishes me luck before reminding me to bury her deep. He calls the dog. She runs by his side as he pedals down the sidewalk. I slide my ticket in the aquatic funeral home pocket of my only brown corduroys. The airport is a far walk across town.

The wind has picked up and the stars are more visible than earlier. I exit the alley as a woman in an electric wheelchair passes by, nearly crushing my left foot. The night sky of Allah romances my steps. Across the street, a neon sign in the window of a mini-mart is advertising their twenty -four hour convenience shopping. In the fading distance of a police siren, I can hear the soliloquy of America's last true cowboy:

"Oh you'll be soup for Uncle Sam's Injuns. It's beef, heap beef, I hear them cry. Git along, git along, git along little dogies. You're going to be beef steers by and by."

Ed's Got Syphilis

"In the arena of human life, the honors and rewards fall to those who show their good qualities in action" - **Aristotle: 384-322 B.C.**

1

She stands three feet from the camera. Her blouse is slightly unbuttoned as her twisting shoulders expose the tension of the scene. Sandra walks backwards toward the bathroom door. Each movement is followed by the camera. Her eyes are a deep green and her fingernails are painted a light shade of orange. A soft layer of ballet music will be edited in as she caresses the brass door handle and walks toward a cast iron bathtub with flowing water and a large quantity of bubbles.

Her direction is to move naturally and provide as much anticipation for the viewer as possible. Sandra releases her top and slides out from her flannel shorts. She gently tests the temperature of the bathwater with her feet before she anxiously guides her legs into the bubbles. Her back is arched as she positions herself in the tub. The camera focuses closely on her facial expressions while she becomes accustomed to the warmth of the bath.

The scene then shifts to the interior of an automobile. William is dressed in a white shirt with a loosened green necktie. He speaks on a cellular phone as he drives quickly through a suburban neighborhood. The vehicle approaches a stop sign.

"Come on, pick it up."

Sandra reaches outside the tub for a cordless telephone set on the towel rack. Her breasts are slightly exposed in her movements.

"Hello."

"I'm running late, but I'm on my way. Don't get all worked up before I get there."

Sandra moves her tongue softly along the receiver, then hangs up the telephone. Her hands disappear into a section of bubbles. Her eyes close dramatically as the scene ends and the music filters in again.

2

The final pieces of the third film are almost in place. The bathroom scene had to be filmed a fourth time this morning. William and Sandra portray their

20

characters with the complete perfection of art and entertainment. Their talents and determination have assisted in all aspects of this production.

William was at one time the voice for *Shorty* on the *Animation Forest* cartoon show during the later half of the 1980's. Most television fans remember his character, which should be a great intrigue for the segment of population that has since rejected our cinematic techniques.

Sandra is beautiful. The curves of her thighs and the acute sharpness of her breasts match perfectly with her small waist size and long brown hair. William is also figuratively well balanced. Each thrust is a magical dive into the modern age of film and art.

Our budget for special effects has increased significantly since the last film. The scene in the burning bedroom was done almost entirely with computer graphics on a specially designed stage with stunt professionals.

The film has officially been titled *Ace In The Whole*. William and Sandra play a married couple living in the suburbs surrounding the Detroit area. The two are professional thieves, focusing their talents on large department stores and antique jewelry shops. They spend their money indulgently and find many acceptable moments for a variety of interpersonal action along the way. The film follows a tight story line with steady interjections of comedy, romance, and high-class physical encounters. Very little is left to the imagination. All plots and circumstances are revealed in a faultless amount of time. This is the beauty of love. This is the magic of entertainment.

3

After our second film was released, my wife and I purchased a house in downtown Boulder near Pearl Street. The house has two floors and a large porch that overlooks a stretch of fine restaurants with a partial view of the mountains. My brother Ed is assembling a doormat as a belated wedding gift with our names stitched into the fabric. Ed teaches basket weaving once a week at the art museum. He is an overweight man with a thick beard and wire-rimmed glasses. He uses basket weaving as a relaxation tool. Ed claims that the museum is a good place to meet people and to explore his artistic interests.

Our second film, *The Dowry of Anne Franken*, featured the 1996 Miss Virginia as our main character and brought in enough money to cover losses we had experienced in the previous seven years with the business. The film involves the young woman in a series of complicated and erogenous kidnapping situations. She portrays the daughter of a wealthy New York businessman who has an extensive attachment to the ransom money. As our films acquire more celebrities, our acceptance within the public becomes more prominent. We anticipate competition over certain roles when the fourth film goes into production next fall.

4

During the filming of *Ace In The Whole*, the crew and I began a new pattern throughout production. For the first time, scenes were shot out of sequence to provide a better time allocation between settings. The scene on Lake Michigan with the yacht was filmed partially on eight millimeter to add the historical touch of adult video.

As the production company takes the time to finalize the last few scenes and work on the audio segments, we are slowly becoming more popular with the media critics and our presence has become moderately respected. Some of the smaller towns on the East coast have started showing our two earlier films after midnight with an *R* rating. The national tendency to reject the forbidden is beginning to decrease as we take giant steps forward into the public art scene.

The promotions crew is having t-shirts printed from *Ace In The Whole*. Plastic action figures are planned for release in adult video stores next month. Our commercials are shown on cable channels for the first time in twelve years.

5

We began this style of cinema in 1986. Our first film was shot for under $3500. The cast was made entirely from volunteers found in a newspaper advertisement. Myself and other crew members have all had scenes in most of our early films. There was never an official script or a legal contract.

The movies brought us little money. We eventually sold many of the sexual scenes to larger pornographic organizations in Southern California. Portions of the dialog and storylines were later recycled and rewritten into some of our current films.

6

The opportunity and inspiration to develop a cultural and publicly accepted approach to pornography came from a Greco-Roman history course I took at a community college in Denver during the summer of 1995. I had given up my dreams of producing pornographic films after several disappointments in our early work.

I decided to return to school to study Anthropology. I became fascinated with our world and how each of us are shaped and modernized by the culture that surrounds us. During my first semester I made a short film on the life of homeless children in American society.

After my first year at college, I discovered the need and the cultural necessity of an open mind towards sexual activity. In Roman Empires both men and women maintained numerous partners that shared no bond other than the action of sex and personal pleasure. The Greeks used private symposiums as social gatherings involving sexual encounters with large groups of participants. Many deities were involved in both cultures as active contributors to the performances.

My brother Ed visited Rome during his freshman year in college. We used his knowledge for the theatrical scenery and for the validity of sexual scenes. Ed later graduated with an associate's degree in Business Marketing. He is currently the Finance Director for all our films.

7

Our first feature production was centered around a Greek Orthodox Priest living in Syracuse, New York during the early years of the Depression. He began studying the culture of Greece and became deeply interested in sexual intercourse with women. The ideas of sin eventually forced the character to institutionalize himself. The film featured part of the cast who had previously been in the Broadway performance of *The Spectacle*. Ed designed the costumes and assisted with the set construction. The film was an instant success and brought us into public theaters for the first time.

8

A large canopy style bed sits in a room with candles and large pillows covering the carpet. The moonlight can be seen through the lace curtains covering the windows. William moves his legs along Sandra's knees. She gasps and then moans respectively. William quickly removes his shirt and begins to use his tongue to massage the front of her neck.

"Tomorrow should prove rewarding."

"All the plans in order, I assume?"

The couple continues the entanglement of their bodies as each is soon stripped of their clothing. William shuffles himself inside her. Sandra smiles and secures her legs tight around William. The motion of the mattress vibrates a small table at the end of the bed. The camera focuses on a large candle as it falls from the table and lights fire to the fabric surrounding the bed frame. William and Sandra appear unaware. The scene fades to black with the sounds of heavy guitar music.

9

A large amount of money and time have been invested in *Ace In The Whole*. It has been our highest cost production since we began. Most of the profits from our two previous releases have helped support this endeavor. According to Ed, we have the potential to earn a fair amount of money from the movie.

My wife and I share a sexual scene in the film. We are placed as participants with non-speaking roles on the yacht. This is our first performance together. It is an untraditional celebration of our success in the industry. The love is real and unrehearsed. Possibly a first in the business.

My wife is highly supportive of my career choice. We have been together for three years. She has seen the production company at its worst, and is now admiring us at our finest. We were married last December in a small ceremony outside of Los Angeles. White doves were released as we exited the courtyard. Ed played the violin and read a short speech at the reception.

10

We have been in discussions all week regarding the circumstances involved in the release of *Ace In The Whole*. Our sound crew is displeased with some of my music selections and the graphics manager has been attempting to make unnecessary additions to some of the action scenes.

William has been complaining about the resemblance of his action figure for the past month. He feels the shoulders are too wide and the hair color is inaccurate. He refuses to have the product released. This is a major production and all pieces need to be in place and in agreement before we can release this as a team. Some of the crew and actors disagree with the use of ballet music in the bathroom scene. They believe it adds an adolescent tone to the film. My intention is to generate a symbol of grace and beauty to the setting and to the characters. Ed suggests that I take full control and have my way with all final decisions. He doesn't understand that this began as a small group of individuals devoted to the establishment of a cultural documentation of sexuality and an intense commitment to fine art.

11

"And the muscular structure is totally wrong. I'm bigger than that."

William stands up from his chair as he speaks. The group of us is silent. Our promotions director appears unconcerned. Ed pays no attention to the remark. I remain in my chair as I address the situation.

"William, these figures have been test marketed by a firm in California specializing in film merchandise. Each aspect of the characters has been designed in a manner that was approved by a selection of typical movie consumers."

"Well if these so-called typical consumers can't tell the difference between a plastic reproduction, then maybe we should reconsider the approach in our target audience."

"The majority of us around this table have a great deal of history in the business. We've seen it from all perspectives and the basic outline has always been to produce great cinema. Right now, we don't have the resources to completely reanimate your figure. You should have said something when we showed you the original two months ago."

"A black and white drawing isn't really an estimate of the final outcome. And besides, when I mentioned something about the rose petal scene, it was overlooked and the idea still ran through. This entire production has been micromanaged by your little regime of under qualified film students and uneducated family members."

William begins to walk around the room as he speaks. The professional atmosphere has begun to weaken. Ed appears nervous as William stops directly behind his chair.

"This is not another *Ann Franken* here. This film means a lot to me. I still have people approaching me on the street asking me to do the *Shorty* voice. I want to overcome that. My skill as an actor has always gone unnoticed. Try to understand me; I refuse to reshoot another scene until these matters are straightened out. You can't do this without me."

I acknowledge his previous sentence with a slight motion of my head. All the others in the room remain quiet. Ed taps his foot against the floor.

"Is it money you want? Tell me what we need to do."

"I just want the respect I deserve. My performance has been demanding and the hours have taken my life away."

"It comes with the business, but if we can help you financially I'll see what can be done."

I make a quick glance at Ed before he answers the question. He appears uneasy. William sits down and pushes the chair away from the table to cross his legs. Ed licks his bottom lip before he speaks.

"I don't think we can handle another cast allowance. The numbers are already going down as we approach deadline."

"I thought things were looking good."

"Thomas, we need to hold on to what little capital we have to put this out for the public. Our monetary plan is dependent on the first week of sales."

William slowly pushes back his chair and steps away from the table. He says nothing as he exits the room. We sit patiently for a moment, expecting his return. Ed resumes his tapping against the floor.

12

"What about the bank loan and the grant from the art institute?"

"Both are gone, all we have left is our personal investments and some of what we made from *Franken*."

The others in the group disperse quiet conversation among themselves. I examine my coffee. It is nearly empty. I close my hands tightly around the cup.

"What does that leave us with?"

Our assistant finance manager exhales softly and stretches his back on the chair. He rummages through a large folder and presents me with a printed copy of our current budget with a brief summary of the expense report for *Ace In The Whole*. Ed quickly gathers his notes and walks out the door, stopping briefly to tighten his shoelaces.

The numbers appear to be in line with the budget. The only unpredicted costs are a few rental fees and food expenses. The assistant manager sits patiently as I look over the remaining papers. He places his pen in his shirt pocket and sits straight in his seat.

"Ed's got syphilis."

The uncomfortable situation is escalated as he speaks to all of us with exaggerated hand movements and a shifting posture. He reaches across the table to retrieve the expense report. He tears the paper into three pieces.

"These reports don't show anything. The numbers have been so disordered for the past few months; I don't know where we stand. Since his first sore turned to a rash, Ed hasn't been doing much of anything to help control costs or estimate spending. He constantly talks about women's magazine articles and afternoon poetry readings at the mall."

"Has he been taking money?"

"I don't know. Maybe. But I don't think so. He's just out of it. Completely uninterested."

"And the syphilis?"

"I think he got it from one of the lighting girls last year."

"The one with the short hair?"

"No, I don't know. I'm just telling you what I heard."

We all sit back in our chairs. The sun has set and the gray of the night has given the room an insensitive blue texture. I call Ed through the intercom. There is no response.

"Have you seen Ed?"

"No."

The same answer is given by everyone in the front office. I search through the file cabinets in the finance department. Receipts and hand written memos clutter Ed's desk. There is an empty bottle of penicillin in his top drawer. I massage my scalp with both hands.

A framed poster of a Greek temple leans against the rear wall. A smaller picture depicting the legend of Romulus has been cut in the shape of a triangle and stapled to the wall in front of his desk. There is a short poem written in black marker on the seat of his chair:

Seasons Change.
Family Remains.
The Constant Battle
Of Blood And Veins.

Ed's coffee mug is stocked with paper clips and business cards. His pencils are perfectly sharpened and arranged in a single line in the order of small to large. I exit the office to refill my coffee in the front hallway. A large man enters through the front door carrying a package and a clipboard. He wears a blue hat with matching pants and a white t-shirt.

"So this is what it looks like inside."

"Excuse me?"

"I have a delivery for a Thomas Starr."

"That's me."

"Yeah, just sign here. Hey, are any of the girls around? This is my last drop."

"Not right now. We're finishing a project."

The man gestures in disbelief and walks out the door with a smile proudly set on his face. I place the small box on the receptionist's desk. My name and business address are neatly written across the front in black marker. I cut the tape with a ballpoint pen. Small pieces of packing material fall from the inside. I pull an intricately weaved doormat from the package. The word *Thomas* is knitted in multicolored yarn across the front. On the underside of the mat, in handwritten letters, is the phrase: *The Constant Battle of Blood and Veins.* There is no accompanying letter or return address.

Ninety Nine Cents and a Self Addressed Stamped Envelope

"You can not judge the significance of hard work through the actions of a group, but rather the desire and success of a single individual. This fact has been proven." - **Sal Martin in his biography: <u>A Win-Win Situation</u>**

1

The lawn is overgrown and the street lights are fading with the approaching sun. The neighborhood dogs are pillaging through the trash. Soda cans and crusted aluminum containers are scattered through the driveway. Chicken bones lie in the street. I can hear the kids on the upper level getting ready for school. My view of the outside is partially blocked by the heavy amber curtains that cover the large front window of our apartment. I can make out a gray image of two neighbors talking on the sidewalk.

I received telephone confirmation last week and the tickets arrived yesterday. The accompanying letter is signed by the show's host in large photocopied writing. The two tickets are the size of index cards and printed with red and black ink. The Shop and Win logo appears on the front with a small advertisement for a free box of cheese flavored crackers if we decide not to use the tickets. There are directions to the studio and a list of hotels included in the package.

Samantha is taking a warm bath this morning. The bathroom door is open and I can hear her singing along to the radio. She brings a tiny bar of soap to her neck and begins to lather herself. Flesh glides roughly across the soap bar, each fold of skin bouncing to the melodies of her bathing.

I scramble eggs on the stove top. Toast withdraws from the toaster perfectly browned. Two glasses of orange juice and today's newspaper sit on the kitchen table. It is our morning of celebration. Yesterday afternoon we received two tickets to be contestants on America's greatest form of competitive entertainment, *Shop and Win*. The game show airs on cable channel twenty-six at 1PM, Monday through Friday. Contestants are paired as couples and must answer various questions regarding grocery store purchases. If the couple does not know an answer they are taken to a small scale version of a grocery store and must find certain items within an allotted time period to receive points. The contestants with the most points at the end of the half hour show take home a year's supply of groceries and up to eight thousand dollars in cash after taxes.

2

Samantha exits the bathroom fully dressed. She wears a plain black t-shirt and gray sweat pants. Her hair is dyed blonde, revealing some of the natural brown at its roots. She is overweight and smokes cigarettes continuously. Samantha uses light blue eye shadow and an excessive amount of mascara to highlight her eyes.

"How was work Michael?"

"Same as yesterday."

I work third shift as a security guard for Andrews Metal Products Inc., a large industrial corporation on the north side of Youngstown. The company manufactures steel accessories for roadway drainage systems.

AMP Inc. designs and builds adjustable manhole risers and sewer catch basins for compliance with various state asphalt paving regulations. They offer all full time employees a competitive benefit package including a dental plan and retirement program if an individual were to stay long enough to end their career at AMP.

There is not much activity during the night watch. I sit alone in front of a television that is divided into four screens. Each four sets flash continuously in eight second time frames. The television broadcasts the situations and environment of sixteen various sections of the facility. I have never witnessed a crime in the twelve years of my employment.

3

Samantha sits down at the kitchen table. Her skin is flushed from the hot bath. She coughs lightly and smiles. She pushes her chair closer to the table and inhales deeply through her nose.

"What's in those eggs that smells so good?"

"Swiss cheese."

"I called my mother last night and told her again about California."

"What'd she say?"

"She laughed and mumbled something about the evils of television and how if we really want something we're gonna have to work for it and not expect someone to hand it to us."

"She's a Virgo, right?"

"One hundred percent."

Samantha picks at the eggs on her plate. She filters the pulp from the orange juice with her front teeth and places it on a napkin. Samantha looks her best in the morning. The freshness of her voice guides me through the alterations of returning home from third shift.

Samantha is employed part time as an astrology reporter for a monthly entertainment magazine distributed throughout Youngstown and the surrounding areas. She has studied the revolutions of the planetary system and its involvement with everyday life since she was thirteen. Sometimes on the weekends we sit on the front steps of our apartment and watch the stars together. Samantha shows me her favorite star formations and explains their symbolic movements with the changing of seasons. We sometimes drink bottled beer and stay awake until all of the stars have disappeared.

4

Shop and Win is filmed in a small studio in Los Angeles. They film five episodes a day. As contestants we are required to drive ourselves to California early next week. Breakfast and lunch will be donated by sponsoring food companies.

Samantha and I own a 1988 Station Wagon. The front and rear door panels are decorated with metal trim that the design department at the Ford Motor Company has painted to resemble wood grain. The turn signals are broken and the horn does not work. The plush interior is stained from chocolate milkshakes and black coffee. I replaced the spark plugs last week and installed a new fuel filter yesterday afternoon. I change the fluids regularly. The engine is strong and the brakes work well. The car will make it across the country and back without problems. It has been a trustworthy vehicle for the past three years.

The host of Shop and Win is a well dressed white male named Sal Martin. Fifteen years ago he was the main character of a prime time television show where he played an overtly neurotic lawyer who won every case he handled. His wife on the show was a high school English teacher. They lived in the suburbs of Chicago with two teenage daughters who always seemed to find themselves in trouble.

In real life Sal Martin has one wife and no children. He lives in a large house in Pasadena with an indoor swimming pool and three compact cars. He is very handsome and Samantha believes he is an Aquarius because of his strong personality. He has long straight teeth and dark brown hair. Sal Martin presents the winners of Shop and Win with their prizes at the end of the show. He smiles and says, *"Keep on shopping"* at the end of every episode. I have practiced my winning handshake for the past two weeks. It is a firm grasp and I will follow it with a loose hug. Samantha plans to kiss Sal on the left cheek.

5

After breakfast I change from my uniform while Samantha cuts coupons from the newspaper. She clips a fifty cents off coupon for instant gelatin and a buy one get one free coupon for heavy duty garbage bags. This is all part of the training we have endured since our decision to be on the game show. The Shop and Win application was a simple one page form. Within a month Samantha and I were accepted. A self addressed stamped envelope can change lives sometimes.

I bring two calculators into the kitchen as she finishes gathering the discounts. I test the solar power of each. Samantha speaks loudly.

"Ok, the price of a fourteen ounce bottle of ketchup after a twenty cent coupon on double coupon day."

"Name brand or store brand?"

"Name brand."

"One dollar and forty nine cents."

"Your off by six cents. That's still ten points."

6

I can feel the lack of sleep in my brain. We hope to arrive in California one day prior to our scheduled recording so I can rest before the questions begin. Samantha does not have a driver's license, so most of the travel will be controlled by me.

The calculators are functioning properly. Samantha suggests driving to the shops on the east side for a better price comparison. We grab our coats and walk outside. A small gray kitten sleeps on the hood of our station wagon. The cat is frightened by our movements and runs away before we enter the car. Samantha squeezes herself into the passenger seat. The safety belt will not fit around her waist comfortably. The vehicle starts without hesitation. We exit the driveway as I clear the fog from the windshield with my sleeve. Samantha lights a cigarette and turns the radio on. Rock music breathes from the speakers.

7

We arrive at Stan's Grocery as the doughnuts are placed in a glass showcase near the first aisle. The frosting is wet and a sugar aroma fills the store. Bleach is on sale with a large display near the produce section. Different brands of peanut butter are scattered throughout the shelving of the first aisle. We are armed with our calculators and notebook paper.

"They ask questions about the set up of stores."

I tell Samantha not to worry. Most stores are set up in identical formats. There are corporations that analyze consumer purchases and design the store accordingly. Bread is in the last aisle after the frozen foods. Condiments and salad dressings are near the fresh flowers and produce. Speciality cheeses in front of the deli. Bulk foods near the bakery. Magazines near the health care products. The expensive items are placed on the shelves at eye level. It is a system of organization and design based on the habitual purchasing methods of the average customer.

Samantha places various items in our shopping cart. She writes down the actual shelf price as I estimate and add my total on a calculator.

"Two ninety nine for a sixteen ounce box of Rice Krispies. Deli cut salami, two forty nine a pound."

"Don't forget to include our coupons."

I multiply percentages and subtract dollar amounts from my total. Samantha takes notes on certain aspects of the store. She writes down the safety precautions of the child's seat in our shopping cart and the average weight of one pull from the bulk dispenser of dried bananas. I examine that sanitation requirements of the seafood department and the pack size of frozen waffles.

The employees at Stan's watch us closely as we inspect the dates on fresh baked bread and compare the differences between red and white grapefruit. We fill our shopping cart halfway then proceed to the checkout. Samantha takes notes on the cashiers scanning procedures.

There is an older woman with short gray hair in front of us in line. She purchases three cans of tomato paste and one white onion. As she leans over the counter to write a check I can see that she wears nothing under her thick green sweater vest. For a moment I have a clear view of her aged breasts. The nipples have swollen and the beauty has faded. I become slightly aroused as she writes a check for three dollars and eighty-four cents. My estimation would have earned fifteen points.

The cashier makes occasional eye contact with us as our groceries are escorted down the rubber belt. She caresses her dry lips while weighing our produce selections. She examines a chart for the PLU number of yellow squash.

"4784."

The cashier checks the validity of Samantha's statement and continues to scan our purchases as I help bag the groceries. Consistent and uniform bagging exercises are sometimes required on the game show.

A final total of eighty seven dollars and fifty two cents is shown on the screen of the register. Samantha rummages through her purse, taking out the coupons. Our total is reduced by three dollars. Samantha routinely waits for me to produce the money for the purchases as I show the cashier my empty pockets. Samantha squeezes through the check out line. The groceries sit neatly packaged in small plastic bags.

"I think I left my wallet in the car. We'll be right back."

We calmly exit the store towards the parking lot. Samantha lights a cigarette and we drive away with the satisfaction that I was only two dollars and fifty cents off from the actual total. Another ten points.

8

For the last year and a half Samantha has been taking Ephedrine pills to control her weight problem. Ephedrine is a stimulant commonly used to treat bronchial infections. Its ability to increase body temperature and improve circulatory functions also make it useful for weight loss and fatigue. The medicine has been banned in certain states due to its association with high blood pressure, breathing difficulties, and heart failure.

I have also become slightly addicted to the drug. It has been a helpful tool during my nights at AMP. Samantha has recently tripled her intake of Ephedrine as we near the scheduled recording date of Shop and Win. She hopes to lose thirty pounds before we are broadcasted on pre-recorded television.

Last week we bought new outfits to wear on the game show. I chose a blue collared shirt with loose fitting corduroys and a matching leather belt. Samantha will wear a yellow sun dress with a gold necklace and white shoes. She hopes to be discovered for her talents as an astrologer during the filming. She has constructed a 1945 version of an Aquarius star chart for Sal Martin and hopes to present it to him before the show. I plan to use the prize money to begin a subsidiary of the AHA in Youngstown.

9

The day is cloudy and most of the leaves have fallen from the trees. We drive two miles to the next training station. *Fantasy Foods* is a large chain store with twenty one aisles of food, health, pet, and cleaning products. They also have a large bakery and a video rental department. We enter the store with the same militant approach as we have for the past month. This training is a serious endeavor in the future of our lives.

There are large displays set up in the front corridor near the shopping carts. The colors contrast beautifully against the wallpaper and tile floor. The discounted products are set up in geometrical arrangements to seduce the shoppers into buying cardboard containers of powdered hot chocolate mix and various other items. We place a one liter bottle of club soda in our cart and proceed to the interior of the store.

10

I received a telephone call at the beginning of the year from Marcus Samspring, a founding member of the Anti Hotel Association. He explained to me the basic principles and history of the AHA in a twenty minute conversation that has given me a new perspective on life and a new respect for the free enterprise system of America.

The Anti Hotel Association began in 1987 as a result of the alarming increase in the cost of room rentals across the United States. The average price of one night accommodations in a single occupancy room have tripled since the economic boom of the late seventies. In an effort to promote good will and equal opportunity, the AHA developed an organized system of self employed individuals located in thousands of cities throughout the world that invite travelers to stay in their residence for a minimal fee. It is a successful business venture for the host and a cost efficient opportunity for the customer. The AHA participant pays a sum of money to the main office and in return receives official window decal's, AHA banners for the front yard, and most importantly a phone number and address listing in the international version of the Anti Hotel Association Magazine, a monthly index of the names and information of all participating members of the AHA. Any individual with the need of a low cost shelter while traveling for business or pleasure can stay for a reduced rate in the home of any member of the organization. For each night that a customer stays in an AHA establishment, they receive a certain amount of points depending on their geographical location. The points can then be redeemed at anytime for a variety of prizes from the Anti Hotel Travelers Catalog.

Samantha and I have an extra bedroom in the rear of our apartment. It can easily be converted into an area of financial growth and hospitality.

11

Fantasy Foods is alive with shoppers as the early morning elderly crowd slowly dwindles out the automatic glass doors. The sliding doors operate by a motion sensor located on a small floor panel or an overhead device. Some stores also offer stationary doors which must be opened and closed by a human hand. These doors are usually placed to the left of the automatic doors to create a sense of security in customers who feel the need to physically open the door as a voluntary reaction to the growing confusion of technology.

"Don't you think this store is a little over priced Michael?"

"Well, I've heard the cost of living in California is slightly higher than Eastern Ohio. So this might be a good price comparison."

Samantha and I assign each other different sections of the large store. She surveys aisles one through nine along with the deli, bakery, and meat departments. I stock the cart with items from the frozen and dairy sections along with aisles ten through fourteen. This mechanical process categorizes and edits the essential knowledge needed for later reconfiguration in our brains.

Aisle ten is filled with dried pasta and ready made tomato sauces. There is a small Jewish section next to the egg noodles. I pull boxes of flavored pasta mixes and jars of chicken broth to the inside of the shopping cart. I quickly enter numbers into the calculator.

My determination is beyond its peak. In two days we will leave Youngstown across highway 76 towards a welcoming path of dreams and expectation.

The aisles are beginning to look the same in each grocery store we encounter. At times it seems as if my body can only function properly when I am calculating the price per ounce of three bean soup or determining the physical differences between various grades of beef.

I am tired of my career at AMP and tired of the ridiculous mental strengthening it has taken to possibly gain a small amount of personal freedom. I sometimes have disturbing dreams involving UPC codes and large plastic containers of pimento cheese.

I am tired of the ninety nine cents attached to the price of most products. Why not simplify the process by rounding the numbers to the nearest dollar and fifty cents. The ninety nine deceives no one.

12

I can picture the first guest at our AHA. He sleeps peacefully in cotton bed sheets while his head rests softly on an over sized pillow. Paintings of deer and small western towns will decorate the wood paneled walls. I plan to install a private toilet with shower facilities off the rear of the bedroom. Samantha will serve a light breakfast in the mornings and provide daily horoscopes for a small fee. I will be able to sleep at night time and eat lunch on a weekday afternoon for the first time in twelve years.

13

There are loud voices coming from the opposite end of the grocery store. I can hear a clutter of shoes running across the hard floor. A distorted female voice transmits on the *Fantasy Foods* loud speaker.

"Mr. Robertson to the bakery. Mr. Robertson to the bakery."

The girl's voice is breathless and afraid. I turn around and push my cart towards the bakery. Two cashiers run in front of me. Their blue aprons float gracefully in their awkward prancing.

There is a small circle of shoppers in front of the bakery. Samantha lies face up between them on the cold tile floor. There is a young man with a light brown shirt and wire framed glasses holding Samantha's wrist with his hand. He has the left side of his head on the center of her chest. He stops occasionally to inspect the clock on the bakery wall and count quietly to himself. I can see her chest rise up and down with short inconsistent breaths. I rush to her side. The brown shirt man pushes me away before I can speak.

"Did someone call an ambulance? What happened? Is she going to be ok?"

The man continues the rhythmic motion between his hand and the bakery clock. An older woman tells me the paramedics are on their way. I sit quietly at the edge of Samantha's feet. My head feels distracted and light. I think about California and swiss cheese. My vision becomes cloudy as I massage Samantha's toes. I realize again that I am tired and in need of sleep.

14

The ambulance arrives as Samantha begins to struggle for air through her nose. The brown shirt man quickly steps away. Samantha lies on her back coughing and rolling slowly from side to side. Her notebook sits behind her head with a blue pen in the spiral binding. She looks at me and says nothing. Her face is pink. Her breathing is quick and uncontrolled. The paramedics transport her large body onto a long plastic board. They carry Samantha out the sliding doors into the rear of the ambulance. Red lights are flashing and the equipment inside the van is bright and full of plastic tubes and small buttons. A crowd of curious shoppers follow us outside. The man who appears to be Mr. Robertson speaks to the driver of the ambulance before they escort her to Saint Elizabeth Hospital.

One of the paramedics informs me that Samantha should be fine and will need to be kept under doctor's supervision for two or more days. Her breathing and heart functions are irregular and her blood pressure is abnormally high.

I return to the bakery department to collect Samantha's purse and notebook. The woman at the counter asks me if I am going to be alright and if I need a ride to the hospital. She has a small birthmark on the left side of her neck. She offers me a warm danish.

"I'll be fine, Thanks."

I walk down aisle three with its shelves stocked full of cookies, fruit drinks, and various snacks. I open Samantha's purse and take out our Shop and Win tickets. Sal Martin's signature looks respectably neat with short and tightly connected letters. He does not place a dot over the I in his last name.

I approach the express cash register as customers in front of the line allow me to pass. I hand the cashier the two tickets and walk slowly through the stationary door toward my reliable automobile. I place the two boxes of cheese crackers neatly in a small paper bag on the yellow fabric of the passenger seat.

Lazarus Milkshake

"I say unto you, I am the door of the sheep. All that ever came before me are thieves and robbers." **John 10:8-9**

1

Floral print bed sheets cover the windows of the upstairs apartment. The carpeting in the living room is scattered with cigarette burns from past tenants. A portable heater warms the entire residence. Jack Crosby sits in a plastic lawn chair at the kitchen table. His long hair is tied behind his head with a blue rubber band. He studies a flyer from a yard sale that will take place this morning one block from his apartment. There will be televisions, children's bicycles, assorted tools, and men's clothing: shirts size large, waist size thirty-four.

He turns around to read the label of his jeans for the second time to be sure that he too is a size thirty-four. He confirms his assumption and walks into the bedroom.

Jack will begin a new job in two hours. He has been unemployed for the past three months. Jack is single and has not been in a serious relationship with a woman in six years.

2

Jack takes the brown leather wallet from his dresser and places it in the pocket of his denim jacket. He turns off the television in the kitchen and walks out the front door.

Jack arrives at the yard sale and immediately focuses his attention to the large pile of men's clothing scattered on top of a wooden picnic table. He shuffles through collared shirts and fleece sport coats. Jack notices a blue pair of pants with the original tags still attached.

"Those are three dollars. I don't know why he never wore those. His sister bought him those two years ago, on Christmas."

Jack turns around and has a good look at the woman speaking. She is an older woman wearing a blue and white horizontally striped shirt and dark glasses to protect her eyes from the sun. She is short and has dark hair unevenly tucked under a white knitted hat.

Jack smiles and continues his search through the clothing. He will also need a shirt, preferably one that will look good with blue pants. The old woman approaches Jack.

"You know, that television over there still works. Fine picture, just needs a remote control. My son said I could pick up one of those universal remotes and it would work just the same. Fine picture though and it doesn't need an antenna."

"How much for this shirt?"

Jack holds up a white shirt with long sleeves and blue buttons on the front pockets. He notices a slight layer of hair on the left side of the woman's face.

"With those pants I'll take five dollars, no less."

Jack hands the woman five dollars and returns to his apartment to change clothes before leaving for work.

3

Jack was raised in Albion, Pennsylvania, in the North Eastern corner of the state. He was born twelve years before the tornado in 1985 damaged his family's home. After arranging minor repairs to their home, his mother and father used a portion of the insurance money to buy an ice cream shop in the town of Girard. It was a small store at a busy intersection near a popular boat access along the Southern shore of Lake Erie. The store was kept open in the months of May through September. Jack worked there as a child sweeping floors and giving his own self-educated opinions to customers on certain flavor combinations of soft serve.

When Jack was twelve years old he was helping his father repair one of the store's three countertop milkshake machines. During a routine cleaning cycle, the interior of the machine was filled with soap and water and then turned on for an hour to sanitize the moving parts. Jack was usually behind the machine with a razor blade peeling a month's collection of dried sugar from the stainless steel cover. As Jack sat on the countertop, one of the bolts on the support legs collapsed bring the weight of the machine directly on top of Jack's right hand. The corner pierced halfway through Jack's thumb before the machine fell off the counter. Jack hit his head on the ceramic tile floor of the ice cream shop. The impact of the machine on Jack's small chest fractured one rib and left him unconscious. After four hours in the hospital Jack woke up with a large bandage on the back of his head and a partial right thumb.

He has since been known to friends and family as Lazarus, from the name of the Christian Biblical character who was able to return from death with the assistance of Jesus. To Jack, the name has certain spiritual qualities that he perceives to play a significant role in his current and future existence.

Shortly after the accident, Jack's father attempted to file a lawsuit against American Creamery Products, Inc., the manufacturers of the equipment that had nearly murdered his son. It was soon discovered that the machine was beyond its warranty and had never been properly serviced according to the manufacturer's recommendations. Rumors began to circulate around the small town that Jack's father had known about the defective machine and had purposely placed his son in a life-threatening situation to avoid the high cost of sending another child to college. At that time, Jack's older sister had recently graduated from nursing school at a large hospital in Erie. The two-year medical program had cost Jack's father a large amount of the family's savings and had nearly put the business out of operation.

A year after the incident, as the rumors grew and became accepted fact, Jack's mother left the family and went to live with her sister in Toledo, Ohio. She never remarried and later died as a result of injuries she experienced in an automobile accident caused by two students returning home for the weekend from Bowling Green University.

4

A & H Targets operates out of a small brick building located two miles from the coast of Lake Erie. The building was once used as the associate headquarters of a small labor union that provided representation for the local chapter of bread workers. A 1974 calendar from a North Dakota wheat farm still hangs on the wall in the break room above the time clock. A photograph of the union's vice president remains behind a glass frame on the rear wall of the target factory. The photo is discolored and is beginning to develop mildew around the edges. The owners Al Bannister and his brother Harold have attempted to maintain the atmosphere of the labor union through its years of archery target production. The company offers its employees no benefit package other than a paid lunch and no drug testing. The calendar and photographs are kept in their original location to represent and remind the employees of the sanctity of brotherhood in the workplace.

A & H Targets produce an assortment of archery targets. The majority of production is concentrated around heavy foam squares that are covered with a vinyl casing that has been screen printed with a circular target pattern set in the traditional red ink. Their products are distributed in sporting good outlets and army surplus stores throughout the United States and Northern Mexico.

5

The wind is directly on Jack's face as the bus door opens. He steps out near the end of the gravel road that leads to A & H Targets. A large wooden sign with the name of the business decorates the path towards the building. Jack puts a newspaper under his arm and walks toward the shop. The distance appears farther than he thought. The morning is cloudy and cold. Birds sing in the background of the leafless oak trees. Jack speaks to himself as he approaches the front door of the factory:

Things are good. Things are great.
Jesus come, Please don't wait.

I'll try my best, I guarantee.
All good things, will come to me.

Hear me Lord. For when I die
Things are good, up in the sky.

The words are a segment of a poem written by Sister Joanne Thompson, an elementary school teacher at St. Mark's just outside Albion. The poem has been published in seven different Catholic prayer manuals for children and has received a number of awards throughout the North Eastern coast. Sister Joanne wrote a short musical accompaniment to the piece in 1979. Jack has memorized the lyrics since the third grade when he played the Autoharp in music class at St. Mark's. Jack and a group of other students in the third grade class performed the song on Easter Sunday during the intermission of the fifth grade's reenactment of Jesus Christ and his ascent from the grave outside of Jerusalem. The words comfort Jack, giving him the reassurance to perform his best on his first day at A & H.

6

There is a young woman behind a glass window sitting at a desk in a small office. The walls surrounding her are decorated with plaques and trophies from the company's softball team. There is a large photograph on the rear wall of a man holding two deer by their antlers. A small, hand painted sculpture of a horse sits on the young woman's desk.

"Hi, my name's Jack Crosby. I'm here to see Al. I'm supposed to start work today."

Jack stands in front of the glass window as the girl motions her head in approval. He sits down in a heavily cushioned blue chair near a small table full of newspapers and magazines.

"Mr. Crosby, just go straight through that door and Al's office is the third door on the right. He'll be there in just a minute."

"Thanks."

Jack walks through the hallway and enters Mr. Bannister's office. There is a radio playing soft orchestral music on top of a bookshelf in the far corner of the office.

Al enters the room and immediately extends his right hand, which is met by the four-fingered hand of Jack Crosby. Al lowers the volume on the radio while stretching his back.

"Mr. Crosby, Jack. How are things?"

"Good."

"Glad to hear that. Well, we need to finish filling out your paperwork and I'll hand you over to Lazarus, and he'll show you what to do. He's been here since we began."

"Lazarus?"

"Yeah, he's one of the best men we've got. He holds the current record for daily production. And he can fix a vehicle better than any man I've seen. He can take a pile of metal and transform it into a high performance piece of machinery. He installed a new transmission in my truck last month. He brings cars back to life, so we gave him the name Lazarus, years ago. The crazy thing is, now he's practically taken target manufacturing into an art form. He carved me that Yorkshire on the window sill. He uses six pound and carves things from it. You might of seen the horse on Sonja's desk up front. That's his. I think he even paints some and sells them at the flea market during the summer."

Jack sits down in a blue chair similar to the one in the waiting area. Al smiles and quickly locates a folder in the file cabinet. Jack can see his first and last name on the tab of the yellow folder. The papers are placed in front of him along with a blue pen and a small telephone book.

"You can take your time filling these out. I'll be back in a few minutes with your gear."

The yellow folder lies face up in front of Jack. He glances down at his new shirt and pants. He notices the color of his pants and the buttons on his shirt match perfectly with the chair he sits in. He opens the folder and begins to fill in the highlighted sections of a *W-4* form.

7

Mr. Bannister returns with a large pair of black rubber gloves and two sets of plastic goggles fastened with adjustable green straps. He smiles and sits in the chair behind his desk. Al quickly explains the correct procedure for tightening the elastic strap of the goggles. Jack takes the equipment and signs his name on the final paper in the folder. A slightly overweight man wearing white leather cowboy boots and a black nylon jacket enters the office.

"Jack, I'd like you to meet Lazarus. He's gonna take you in the shop and get you started."

Lazarus stands about a foot lower than Jack. He makes direct eye contact with him as they shake hands. Jack notices an uncomfortably tight handshake. Lazarus scratches his scalp with his free hand.

"Nice to meet you Crosby. This is a great place. A lot of good, hardworking men here. It's a pretty simple job once you get it down. Probably won't take you too long."

"Sounds good. I'm ready when you are."

Al motions his head in approval and rolls his chair back a few feet to stretch his legs on the floor. Lazarus leads Jack out the door towards the work area. Jack can hear the sound of men talking behind the vibrations of machinery at the end of the hallway. Lazarus walks with large, exaggerated steps. His name is airbrushed in red and gold lettering on the back of his jacket. There is also a design of a large blue automobile surrounded by an embroidered cloud of smoke on each sleeve.

8

The shop is smaller than Jack had imagined, with white brick walls and a polished concrete floor. There are five other men working at various stations throughout the room. Each man looks absorbed in their labor with occasional conversation shouted at each other in reference to production par levels and stories of their lives outside of A & H Targets.

Lazarus escorts Jack past a short assembly line with two men quickly filling and shaping printed vinyl bags with heavy foam. Each man has a set of industrial scissors to cut the required length of packing material. They stand quietly, making quick glances at Jack as he walks by.

"This will be your station for today. We'll see how it works for you. The last guy had a hard time keeping up with par."

"So I just sort of do what they're doing?"

Lazarus smiles with his lower lip and with the tightening curve of his chin. He uses a small white cloth to remove the sweat from his forehead.

"Well, it's a little more complicated than that. You gotta get each one to the right size and make sure that each bag is completely filled with no uneven edges. And you gotta make sure the printing is centered on front of the target."

Lazarus stops talking to scratch the lower portion of his neck and provides Jack with a sheet of thick woven vinyl stitched into the dimensions of a small 2X2 target.

9

Jack soon learns that Lazarus rents an apartment by himself three blocks from the factory and collects antique motorcycle parts and custom builds snowmobiles. He is familiar with the ice cream store that Jack's father operated in Girard. His family had been there many times during summer outings to the lake. He remembers eating chocolate sundae cones on picnic tables in the parking lot. Lazarus owns three cats and is currently rebuilding an outboard motor for a fishing boat. Earlier this year his father passed away following three months in the hospital with pneumonia. His mother has recently been diagnosed with AMD in her left eye. She has difficulty driving a car and needs to regulate her exposure to the sun.

Jack instantly befriends Lazarus as he becomes accustomed to the machinery and the tedious task of measuring the material. After lunch Jack is working at the same pace as the others and has kept up hourly par levels along the way.

"I've never seen someone pick up so fast, you look like you've done this before."

Lazarus scratches the side of his head and continues his work. Towards the end of the workday most of the men remain quiet. Jack becomes respected for his level of production and the ability to work despite the slight limitations of his right hand.

10

At the end of the day Jack is invited to join the others for a drink at a bar near the shop. The production crew meet there everyday after the shift is done. The bar is a dark place with draft and canned beer. They also sell a limited selection of liquor and white wines. Jack selects a stool placed close against the bar. Lazarus sits beside him and buys the first round of drinks for all the workers. This time of the year, the output at A & H is at its maximum. They toast to the nearing end of hunting season, when production will cease for five months while they collect unemployment until spring.

Jack observes one of the other workers near the end of the bar attempting to impress the bartender with misleading stories and the distinct sound of responsive laughter. Lazarus explains to Jack the problems he's having with rebuilding the clutch of a 1989 Yamaha motorcycle. Jack stays quiet, listening to the conversations around him. He drinks slowly while Lazarus uses a thin straw and a damp cocktail napkin to demonstrate the procedure he uses to shape discarded foam into figure art. Jack orders himself another beer as Lazarus pauses to scratch the back of his neck.

"You know Jack, I think you're gonna like working with us. It's like one big family. Five days a week. We all watch out for each other."

"What's there to watch out for?"

"Lots of things, the world we live in, you never know what could happen. Gotta keep your guard up at all times. And if it falls, you got all of us to stand behind each other."

Lazarus orders a pitcher of beer and takes off his jacket, exposing a tattoo of a small angel on the interior of his right arm. He refills Jack's glass then gives him a quick wink as he stares into the mirror behind the small arrangement of liquor bottles. Jack watches Lazarus as his thick body attempts to keep posture on the barstool. Jack keeps eye contact with him as he drinks his beer.

"You ever read the Bible, Lazarus?"

Lazarus squints his eyes and sips at his drink. He looks at Jack's reflection and places his glass on the wooden countertop. The brief silence is interrupted by a familiar song playing on the jukebox in the back room. Lazarus begins to whistle along with the music. He closes his eyes for a brief moment.

"I went to church as a kid and I know a lot of the stories but I never really sat down and read everything. I believe in God. That's all I need."

Jack fills his glass again and continues the conversation as Lazarus looks toward the end of the bar where the others have begun a game of darts.

"There's a story in the Book of John where Jesus says to his disciples: *I seek not my own glory, There is one that seeketh and judgeth. If a man keep my saying, he shall never see death."*

Lazarus stands up from the barstool. He twists his neck in an awkward motion and takes a large swallow of beer.

"Sounds about right."

"Yeah, the Bible has been a big part of my life since I lost this."

Jack holds his right hand in the air and gives Lazarus a brief history of his family and the accident at the ice cream shop. He begins to talk about his father's current situation.

"He's been on Social Security for the past few years, he lives here in Girard in a small house near Hathaway."

Lazarus arches his back and twists his neck again. He seems uncomfortable with the family history of the Crosbys. He orders another pitcher and asks Jack to join him for a game with the others.

"Well, I gotta catch the last bus that lets off near my house. It runs through here in about twenty minutes."

Lazarus pushes the bar stool against the wooden counter. He fills his glass, then approaches Jack.

"You need a ride back to your place? We can play one game, then I'll take you home."

Lazarus stands a few feet from Jack. His nostrils motion with every breath. Jack sips slowly, then nods his head in an appreciative gesture.

"Sure it's no problem?"

"Hey, you see the sleeves on my coat? That's what you'll be ridin' in."

Jack corrects his posture and studies the designs on the jacket. He also appears uncomfortable with the situation. He looks intently at the smoke clouds and the car on the sleeves.

"Really? I think my dad's got an old car that looks something like that. It's a dark red though. Hasn't had it running in about two years. Sits in the backyard with flat tires."

Lazarus stops his movements to scratch the top of his shoulders. The sweat stains under his arms appear to be a permanent design on his t-shirt. He looks at Jack and tilts his head to the right, inhaling deeply. Lazarus simulates the throw of a dart with his right hand.

"A prospective Impala, let's take a look."

11

On the drive towards Jack's father's house, Lazarus explains to Jack his concept of establishing his own archery target business. Lazarus drives a 1973 Chevy Impala. The interior has been replaced with blue leather seat covers and a wooden dashboard dramatically shaped and polished to match the curves of the exterior of the automobile.

"Yeah, I ran the idea past Al and Harry a year ago. They don't see any money in it. You know I think people would go for life size foam sculpture. It would take hunters where they've never been before. It would be an intense physical experience for any sportsman. I could create original, three-dimensional targets that resemble what people are after. Bears, eight-point deer, wild pheasant, or anything. I could even make targets of people or things the customers don't like. Politicians and celebrities."

Jack watches carefully as Lazarus moves his neck dramatically between sentences. The conversation seems rehearsed and very authentic.

"It's a new generation of hunters out there. People like me, who have a need for a variation on the traditions of man. Technology is growing, and our society is becoming more advanced everyday. And with the structure of the foam and a tight vinyl overlay, I know this could work. So after I save a little more, I'm gonna buy me a surplus of six pound and rent a small garage down on South Main. Al and Harry won't know what their passin' up."

12

Lazarus continues to express the desire to be self-sufficient through the use of his artistic and mechanical talents. Jack stays quiet as they approach his father's home. It is a paved road with a continuous reflective line that runs through the center, separating each side. Jack's father is a simple man who lives in a small rented house at the end of the street with a large area of woods surrounding his home. His father seldom leaves the house and frequently sits in a wooden chair watching Public Television while drinking ginger ale. The floors of his home are covered with cardboard boxes full of old Christmas cards and automobile magazines. He has two functional refrigerators in the kitchen. After selling the ice cream shop, Jack's father went to work part time at a car lot in East Springfield. He continued working there until he was sixty-five, when he retired and began collecting used furniture that he would reupholster and then sell through newspaper ads.

Earlier in the year he had to have an operation on his lower back, which has convinced him that he will soon join his spouse in the privacy of the after-life. He left the furniture business and discontinued communication with both of his children as he prepares himself for death and the long awaited reunion of his departed love.

"It's up here on the left, but turn your headlights off and park over there by the ditch."

"He's asleep? Yeah, lets roll over here and take a look."

Lazarus grabs a flashlight from under the front seat. He places his arms through the sleeves of his nylon jacket and turns toward Jack. Jack appears calm and uses his hand to motion his friend to the back of the house.

The grass in the front yard appears to be recently trimmed. As they move toward the rear of the house, the weeds and grass become taller. There are identical plastic bird feeders set on short wooden posts throughout the yard. A small pile of rubber tires and an assortment of furniture pieces are positioned under a small shelter near the entrance to the house.

On a corner section of the lawn, surrounded by tall grass sits a 1975 Chevrolet. The exterior has begun to rust and the passenger side door is partially open, revealing the rain damaged upholstery and a small pile of tools on the floor panel. Lazarus stays silent as he circles the car with an arrogant smile beginning to develop on the sides of his mouth.

"My father worked on this car every night after he started at the car lot. It's worse now then when he started."

"It looks like he made some progress with the engine. The belts are still new and the carburetor looks partially rebuilt. I bet if we put some nice wheels on this and rewire the ignition we could probably cruise around the block a few times."

Jack shakes his head in agreement and moves the palm of his hand delicately across the top of the vehicle as he clears his throat. Lazarus continues a personal observation of the engine. His small body is awkwardly bent at the waist as he leans towards the motor. Jack steps back from the vehicle as he speaks. He twists his neck and touches the rear axle of the vehicle with both feet.

"I don't think my father would even notice if we took this car. He hasn't been in the backyard for years. He pays a neighborhood kid three dollars a week to cut the grass in the front yard and to keep the bushes from overgrowing. If we got this out of here and got it going again, how much do you think it'd be worth?"

"I don't know. Completely restored models are going anywhere from fifteen hundred to seven or eight grand."

"You gotta way to get it out of here?"

Lazarus seems apprehensive. His small hands are clasped together and he is slowly beginning to perspire. His boots are easily visible as the moon begins to appear. Lazarus releases a loud sigh.

"Well, I haven't talked to him in a while, but my cousin has a tow truck. Works all right. You sure the old man won't hear us? And how is he not gonna see that a '75 is missing from his backyard?"

"That's where the foam comes in. Six pound, like you said."

Lazarus impatiently scratches the back of his neck and looks at Jack. He appears impressively stout as he begins to massage the front of his face with his right hand.

"Six pound?"

Jack motions Lazarus towards the front of the house. The neighborhood is silent and unaware. Porch lights separate each house from the next. The road has been freshly paved. Loose asphalt pieces are scattered throughout the yard as the two near Lazarus' car.

"So what are you talking about Jack?"

"You think you could sculpt a life size reproduction of it? I could help invest in a block of foam and we could replace the Chevy with a replica. My dad would never know the difference. We could weigh it down on the opposite side. Away from the house. And like I said, he never goes in the backyard. The only time he sees that car is when he's at the window above the sink doing dishes."

Jack is nervous. He is chewing on his bottom lip and blinking his eyelids in a repetitive motion. He can taste the alcohol on the back of his tongue.

"Yeah, but then what do we do with the car? I mean, I don't have room for it and you don't even drive."

"You think you can get it going and fix it? We could split the money and you could use part of it to begin the business and I could start investing my share."

"I don't know. You think it will work? Your father is gonna notice, and why would you want to do this?"

"If we don't trust our fellow men, who is left to assist us when we need it most. The New Testament says: *Greater love hath no man than this, that a man lay down his life for his friend.*"

48

Lazarus acknowledges the wisdom of the biblical passage. He opens the car door and places the seat belt into the folds of the drivers seat.

"Let's get out of here, man."

Jack slides in the seat next to Lazarus. The random sections of light from the television in Jack's father's house cast descriptive shadows across the row of bushes along the porch.

"So what do you think?"

"The problem is the organization of the entire event."

"You think you can sell it?"

Lazarus scratches his left ear with his thumb. Jack sits up straight in the passenger seat. His shirt is slightly unbuttoned. Lazarus reaches into the glove box and takes a small plastic comb to his head.

13

The effects of the beer have passed. Jack stretches his neck and stares out the window at a passing car. Lazarus turns on the overhead light to read the time on his watch.

"It's not even ten."

Jack continues looking out the window at the streetlights and passing cars. He takes a short breath through his nose and cleans his teeth quickly with his tongue. The oncoming headlights are more frequent as they approach the main road. Jack makes shadows on the interior car door with the four fingers of his right hand.

Lazarus signals left. Jack turns off the overhead light and tightens the rubber bands around the back of his hair. He looks up at the clouded stars. His new pants adopt a dark gray color under the moonlight. Lazarus turns slowly into a parking lot.

"My father used to wear shirts like that."

"I like the contrast of the buttons on the pockets."

"My mother tried to give me some of his clothes after the funeral."

The car stops and the two exit the vehicle towards a small restaurant in the main area of downtown Girard. The front door of the building opens easily as the men direct themselves to the young woman behind the cash register. Jack is first in line. They both remove their coats as they approach the counter. Their hands are stained with grease and dust form the Impala. As Jack reaches for his wallet, he turns to read the interior label of his pants to confirm the purchase of a size thirty-four.

Sunrise Special

"A mountain of buttermilk pancakes covered in pure maple syrup with fresh honey-butter, accompanied by two fried eggs, Canadian bacon, and your choice of whole grain toast or a serving of home fries: $4.99." - **Anonymous**

1

The extra pounds of flesh drape themselves from the arms of the large waitress behind the counter. The smell of bacon and vegetable oil floats over our booth. I arch my back against the soft cushion behind me. A young man approaches our table. He is thin with a white complexion. I cannot see underneath his bright yellow uniform. I assume that the remainder of his skin also carries a bright pink tone.

The waiter has large pimples on his chin. He walks toward us with small, evenly spaced steps. He smiles as he takes hold of a notebook.

"Hi there, can I start you off with something to drink?"

"Is this orange juice from concentrate?"

"Yes, I believe so."

Carol acknowledges my assumption and the young man moves towards the next table of customers. I can see that he wears no socks and his shoes are in need of polishing. I can hear him project a similar sentence on the customers behind us regarding their beverage selection. They choose coffee and two glasses of ice water.

Carol appears tired this morning, her eyelids are heavy and the natural aging around her mouth is more visible under the fluorescent lighting that decorates the ceiling above us.

"What are you getting to eat?"

"I'm not sure. Either the Western Omelet or the Belgium Waffles."

"The waffles come with a side of eggs and toast. But I was thinking about getting the Sunrise Special again, with home fries."

Carol is excessively thin, with a pleasant tan this time of year. Her hair is tightly curled and dark. She wears a thick layer of eyeliner and delights in covering her body with a variety of form fitting clothes. Carol is employed by the school district as a student counselor.

I sit across from her as she stretches her back and uses both hands to twist her neck. Carol assembles her hair in an outward motion from her tiny skull. She sits quietly as we await our drinks. The restaurant is busy this morning.

Carol pulls a package of cigarettes from her purse.

"You want one?"

"Not right now. We need to talk."

"Here?"

"Well, if this is going to happen tonight don't you think we should have everything organized and thought out?"

The young waiter approaches our table. His face expresses a slight disorientation. He has a pencil tucked behind his ear.

"Sir, I'm sorry, but did you order yet?"

"No, we didn't."

"Well, can I get you two something to drink?"

"I'll have the milk and bring my wife a coffee."

The young boy writes our order on his notebook paper. We make no mention of our previous drink selection. He smiles and walks to the counter.

2

We have breakfast here every Saturday morning in the summer. The place is near the beach and has reasonable prices. The restaurant is well known for their quick service and for a large breakfast selection. Carol and I walk along the East pier before we eat. She enjoys the morning sun on her skin. She says that it keeps her healthy and young.

"What I was saying was, if we're going to do this tonight, then we should make sure we're completely prepared."

"What, like make a list or something?"

"No. We just need to go over the main things like timing and the possibility of alarms. And exactly where the car will be parked. That kind of stuff."

"Ok, so you start."

The young waiter brings our drinks on a small tray with one plastic straw wrapped in paper. He hands Carol the milk and me the coffee. He leaves as Carol and I exchange our beverages. Carol offers me the straw with a grin perfectly attached to her face.

"Well, we need to do something like synchronize our watches so we're on time. Because for a short period we'll be separated."

"I don't have a watch."

"I thought you said you had an old one you could wear."

"I looked for it yesterday and couldn't find it. It's that digital one my sister got me last year, the one with a metal band and the push button light so you can see the time when its dark."

"Alright, don't worry about the watch right now. Let's go over the entrance and exit positioning."

"Hello again. Have you made a decision as to what you'd like this morning?"

The young man leans on our table, the notebook is tight in his hands and his hair has become slightly out of place. Carol sits up in the seat and opens her menu. She moves her finger up and down on the plastic covering. She bites softly on her tongue.

"I think I'll have the Sunrise Special."

"Did you want toast or a side of home fries with that?"

"Home fries, please."

"And for you, sir?"

"The Western Omelet with toast and a side of bacon."

The young boy looks at another page in his notebook. He laughs softly as he speaks. His front teeth are noticeably whiter than the others.

"I think the bacon is extra."

"That's fine."

He takes our menus and returns to the counter to place our order with the cook. He scratches the back of his neck with a pencil.

3

I recently accepted a part time position at *Murrins Tire and Auto Body*. I assist the dock manager three days a week stocking shelves and unloading shipments. The pay is small but with Carol's extra income from the school district we manage to rent an apartment downtown and recently purchased a used car and a complete living room set. I receive a discount on tires and a free balance and rotation every three months for our car.

"I think we need to make sure the rear entrance is blocked, so nobody can get out the back if anyone is in there. We should park the car by it. There's only two doors and if we block one then we only have to concern ourselves with the front."

"Good idea."

"And we have to remember the cameras. We can't cut the electricity; it might set an alarm. If I go in the backdoor and you park the car, I can get in the office and turn off the VCR and let you in the front with the suitcases."

"I'm hungry. I hope they hurry up."

"Remember, I'm going to need you to set the alarms off at the high school, then meet me at the front door of the store. The police will run over to the school and we'll be in and out with the money before anyone notices."

"How do I set it off again?"

"Just break a window or something. It's a new school; they probably have those window alarms. Just look for a room with a lot of computers or maybe the library or something."

"Ok, then I'll drive back and park by the backdoor and you'll let me in the front, right?"

I nod my head in approval and take a large sip of milk through the straw.

Carol drinks her coffee and looks around at the people in the restaurant. The large woman behind the counter is counting dollar bills and talking with a man seated on a stool near the cash register. Our waiter is taking an order from a couple seated in a booth across the room. Carol turns her head to the table behind us.

"They're already eating, and we sat down before them."

"It's probably the Sunrise Special that's holding things up."

Carol looks at me and says nothing. She plays with her napkin, unfolding it, then folding it again. She begins tapping her fingers on the table in rhythm to the music circulating through the speakers in the restaurant. I rub my eyes and examine the salt and pepper shakers on our table.

"I wonder who thought to put rice inside salt shakers?"

"Probably someone with a lot of time on their hands."

"It takes in moisture and helps the salt come out easier."

"Why don't they put rice in the pepper?"

"I don't know."

4

The young man approaches us again. His pencil is in the front pocket of his uniform . His face appears flushed and his hair is back in its correct location. His yellow shirt is tucked in.

"I'm sorry, but your breakfast is taking a little longer than expected. We usually have two cooks on Saturday but the other guy called off and we're pretty busy, but I'll try to get him to hurry on yours."

"Thank you."

The boy leaves and walks to the front of the counter. He makes gestures with his hands at the cook. The cook says something to him and then shakes his head before returning to the grill to inspect a piece of chicken. The boy asks the large woman behind the counter a question. She laughs and continues to count her money. Carol looks at me and smiles. I notice a thin layer of dirt under my fingernails. I have not showered in two days.

5

"We know the ATM guy restocks the machine near the front door on Saturday mornings, so there should be a good amount still inside by tonight if we can pry it open."

"Why don't we just take the whole thing?"

"They have trackers. If we take it they can locate the machine and we'd be caught."

"I forgot about that. The safe is near the register right?"

"Yeah, it's behind the battery display, next to the cigarettes. It's not a very big once. Shouldn't be too heavy."

"We gotta get a bunch of cigarettes too, don't forget."

"I know, and we'll get some food. Cases of it."

"And beer too."

"Yeah, maybe even a couple bottles of wine. The school alarm should keep them occupied for a while. All we need is twenty minutes."

"I'm excited about all this. Aren't you?"

"Yeah, and I'm getting hungry. I don't think the cook has even started our order yet."

"Are you sure?"

"I haven't seen him crack an egg in the past ten minutes."

"Call that waiter over here again."

"Just wait, it can't be too much longer."

"He's not getting a tip from us, that's all I know."

Carol lights another cigarette. She unfolds her napkin again and places it on her knees. I light a cigarette and take the last sip of my milk. Carol looks around again at the other customers. Her hair is tucked behind her ears as she impatiently sucks at the cigarette.

The young boy carries a plate of pancakes to a man sitting near the window. The man smiles and immediately begins to eat his breakfast. He sits close to the table and straightens his shirt collar. The boy comes toward us again. His motions are quick and awkward. He appears unhappy and visibly nervous.

"You wanted the Sunrise Special and the omelet, right?"

"Yes, the Western Omelet."

"Ok, I think it's ready. I'll be right back."

The boy walks to the counter and speaks with the cook. They shake hands and the cook resumes his work on the grill. Carol rolls her eyes.

"I still don't think it's coming."

"Just wait."

6

The mini-mart is three miles from our house. It closes on Saturday nights at eleven. We have approximately fourteen hours to prepare. I

54

stocked our car with equipment this morning. Carol has been tense for the past two weeks.

"We should get some kind of backup plan don't you think?"

"Carol, I've been thinking about the whole thing for almost a month now. It has to work. Every angle is covered. We just need to get the timing straight."

"I won't take any lessons from that cook over there."

"No, we can stop on the way home and time the drive from the school. Then we'll just set our watches to the exact second."

"I told you, I can't find my watch."

"So, we'll buy a cheap one at the drug store across the street."

"They don't sell watches over there."

"How do you know?"

"Drug stores don't have watches."

"I saw a watch at one the other day."

"It doesn't mean that store is going to have a watch."

"Just listen for a second, I have the whole thing organized. If we just stay with the plan, it will all come together. We'll get a watch somewhere, and tomorrow morning we'll be eating breakfast at *The Montclair* on Third Street."

7

Brown wood paneling covers the walls of the restaurant. There is a ship propeller above the front entrance. Paintings of sailboats and plastic swordfish are scattered throughout the building. Ceramic anchors and other seaside paraphernalia decorate the walls.

"Where is our food?"

"I think he's coming, I just saw him look at us after the cook gave him two plates."

"That's not ours."

I place a cigarette in the ashtray. Carol mumbles something about wanting to leave. I attempt to make eye contact with our waiter. He stumbles to the other side of the restaurant toward a couple seated in a corner by the television. He patiently writes their order on the top page of his notebook. The couple politely acknowledges his response as the young boy returns to the front counter.

"We can probably do it in fifteen minutes if I can get the ATM open."

"I'll get the cigarettes and food, you get the safe. I can't carry something like that."

"Think you can carry one suitcase and the other stuff at the same time?"

"I'll make two trips."

"It will probably be about forty pounds. Just help me look out for police."

Our waiter escorts himself to the far wall near the bathrooms. He sits at a corner table smoking a cigarette and drinking a small glass of orange juice. He reads a section of the newspaper and carefully positions his legs under the table.

"Is he taking a break?"

"I don't know. It looks like it."

Carol leans back against the vinyl booth. She sighs heavily and examines her cigarette pack. The young boy across the room sips at his juice. Carol peels off the cellophane from her cigarettes.

"Who is the Surgeon General anyway?"

"I'm not sure. Someone in Washington, probably a group of people."

"It's not Generals, just General."

"He's lighting another cigarette. Look at him."

"Let's get out of here, we'll just eat at home. We have bacon in the freezer and I can make some eggs."

"He doesn't seem to be in a hurry over there."

"Should we say something? Isn't there a time limit in this place?"

"No, let's just go. They're under staffed anyway."

8

The large waitress instructs us to have a good day as we pass the front counter. I can see the reflection of her smile in the glass door as we exit. The sky is a clear blue. Seagulls float near the lamp posts. The asphalt in the parking lot is freshly paved and the handicap spaces are painted a bright yellow similar to the young boy's uniform. Carol and I walk slowly towards our car. The rear windows are partially open. Carol holds my hand as we walk. She moves the hair from her eyes as she speaks.

"Bacon and eggs should be alright."

"Tomorrow we'll be at *The Montclair*. Fifteen minutes is all we need."

"Are you sure you can shut off the VCR in the office?"

"It's just like a regular VCR, push stop."

"Did you leave the back windows down?"

"Keeps it from getting too hot in there."

"We should buy one of those cardboard things for the front window."

"We still have planning to get done. Do you know what time it is? We need to organize this thing."

"We forgot to pay for our drinks."

Carol opens the passenger side door. She places her purse between both legs as she sits. I place the key in the ignition and start the engine.

Carol moves the visor to shield her eyes from the sun. She rolls down her window and lights a cigarette. I back out slowly from our parking space. The motor roars with excitement.

Rice Paper Wine Glass

"When tides at ease on the evening breeze, and the scarlet moon starts its gentle rise. The drowsy whale spouts a misty trail, and the stars gather slowly in the skies." - **Irving Burgie**

1

The sound of traffic increases as we near Fourth Avenue. The streetlights and neon signage can be seen from where we walk. Annabelle tells me it is a beautiful night. I agree and we continue walking. The sky is a deep gray. She tightens her knuckles and resumes the conversation.

"Don't you think the stars are prettier from where we live?"

"They start to fade in this area."

"Light pollution."

Annabelle hums to herself as we walk. I am unable to recognize the song. The central area of the city is now visible to us. A line of cars can be seen between the side streets. My feet have adjusted to the absence of shoes. A pattern of traffic lights escorts us to the bus terminal. The Arizona air is warm this evening.

A taxi brought us to Lowell Street and we continue to walk the remaining distance. Annabelle is fascinated with the night sky. She claims that history can be told through the constellations. Each star is allegedly a representative of a past life. Animals, humans, and plants become a part of the universe after each of us passes on. Every star and planet is a component of our present and future existence. They guide us and offer protection to those who need it most.

The bus station is a few streets in the distance. Annabelle has been silent for the past few minutes. Her pace has quickened and her breathing has become rhythmic. She walks with one hand behind her back.

"David, do you know how much farther the station is?"

"It's right here at the next light."

"How much time do we have before our bus leaves?"

"Probably twenty minutes."

"Are your feet starting to hurt?"

"They're fully conditioned."

It has been nearly three months since I have worn shoes. The purity of this action has helped me realize the solid temperament of nature that we have attempted to escape through modern technology. We have developed methods of control over our natural environment. Our feet and skin are a connection to the earth; they are the roots of civilization. By protecting our feet with shoes we lose touch with the intimacy of our universe and with our personal belonging on planet earth.

2

As we approach the bus station, Annabelle ingests a large amount of vodka from her flask. She wipes her lips with an oversized shirt sleeve and places the bottle in her purse. She wears a large backpack and her hair is tied in a long braid that floats across her shoulders as she walks. Annabelle gestures her eyes towards my guitar case before she speaks. I smile with the acceptance of our decision.

"Remember when you first got that guitar?"

"And you couldn't stand to hear me play?"

"And now look where it's brought us. It seems symbolic. Especially with the stars tonight."

"We always talked about traveling."

"And you wanted to play guitar."

Annabelle drinks a mouthful of vodka before we enter the bus terminal. A backpack is fastened tightly around my shoulders. Annabelle removes the tickets from her pocket and begins to study our departure and arrival times. I place my baggage on the floor and sit next to Annabelle on a plastic chair in the lobby. The station is crowded. I begin to twist the hairs on my arm as I read a small pamphlet that Annabelle gave me this morning. The brochure is a five-page summary about the rise of Buddhist sects in the Caribbean. It gives the names and addresses of small organizations throughout the islands. There is a brief history of the religion and an assortment of photographs and quotations from founding members in the tropics.

"If St. Martin doesn't work out, we can try one of the other islands. I'm sure I can contact one of the temples and get involved in something. They could help us find a place to live."

The smell of alcohol is thick on Annabele's breath. Her eyes move quickly around the lobby as she speaks. A group of security guards are occupied with a young woman working at the gift shop near our seats. The woman applies a layer of lipstick to her bottom lip. The guards examine my feet and continue their dialogue. I position myself in the chair.

"What makes you think St. Martin won't work out? I've been practicing these songs for the past four months."

"I'm not saying it's not going to happen, I'm saying we need options if the situation should arise."

59

"Just because I'm not a native doesn't disqualify me from my musical abilities."

"That's not what I'm saying, David. It's just that we've both seen you experiment with a lot of great ideas that faced difficulties and had to be reevaluated or completely discontinued."

"Like what?"

"Remember your toy book for cats? With the pages made from hand pressed paper and dried catnip with lemongrass herbs. Most cats couldn't turn the pages. They tore apart the seams with their claws."

"We sold fifty copies, didn't we?"

"And we still lost money."

"It was a good idea."

3

Annabelle stares at the clock on the far wall of the station. It is ten minutes before boarding time and she suggests we stand in line by the door. I mumble in agreement and we walk towards the departure area. Annabelle yawns and rubs her eyes with both sets of fingers. She laughs and then whispers in my left ear.

"And do you remember your idea to end the tampon?"

"I never started that one. It was just a thought."

"An unhealthy one."

"It would probably work."

"Women have to bleed David, it's a natural occurrence in the female body, without it neither of us would be here."

"What about using it on heavy days?"

"No."

"Are you sure?"

"There's a scripture from the Gita that says: *I would enjoy wealth and pleasures stained with blood.*"

"It was a good idea."

I rest my hat slightly over my eyes. Annabelle recognizes the motion and immediately ends the conversation. I hold the handle of my guitar case tightly and look around at the others in line. There are families, various elderly men, and an overweight couple in front of us. Two men next to us speak in Spanish. It becomes difficult to concentrate.

Our bus number is announced on the speaker system. Annabelle tightens her knuckles and hold our tickets in front of her. The line moves in an organized sequence onto the bus. A tall man wearing a dark blue uniform examines our tickets. He tears a portion off, and takes our luggage. I watch him carefully as he places my guitar in the compartment underneath the bus. Annabelle keeps her purse held against her chest. She carries a small suitcase full of books and snack food. She asks me to walk faster so she can sit down.

"Let's go near the back. I want the window seat."

"I hope the bathroom is clean."

"By early morning we should be in Houston and we'll switch seats after the layover."

I assume she will have the window seat the entire bus ride. It will be approximately two and a half days before we reach the airport in Miami. Annabelle needs the window. Her mind has difficulty functioning in small places. The window will keep her occupied. The books will help her relax during the day.

After a lengthy boarding process, the overhead lights dim and the bus backs up. We exit the terminal onto Fourth Street as Annabelle removes the flask from her purse. I take a sip and return the container to her. She laughs and finishes the bottle in two long swallows. I glance back at the bathroom; there is a man in the seat behind me wearing a denim vest covered in decorative patches. He wears sunglasses and holds a flashlight on his lap. I cannot tell if his eyes are open or closed. A young boy sits next to him near the window.

4

We decided on St. Martin after a week of research at the library near our apartment. St. Martin is the smallest island in the Caribbean to be shared by two independent governments. The Dutch and the French have maintained a peaceful coexistence for over three hundred years; the longest in history of two bordering nations. The climate is perfect throughout the year.

I studied magazines about the history of traditional Calypso music and its effects on Caribbean culture. The songs, lyrics, and instruments have been part of the Caribbean lifestyle for years. My attraction to the sound was developed through a number of Jamaican immigrants around the Flagstaff area where I grew up. The sound of conga drums combined with a simple chorus and a fine arrangement of skilled musicians has provided me with the necessary essentials to recreate the sound with a strong appreciation of its history.

I bought an acoustic guitar last year while Annabelle was searching for ceramic ashtrays around neighborhood yard sales. The guitar is designed with a standard wood grain finish with brass tuning keys. I took lessons from a woman across the street from our apartment. Her methods were strict and I later decided to continue my studies alone on the living room couch of our apartment. My progression was slow, but I was able to quickly compose short improvised versions of traditional Calypso performances.

Annabelle fastened a drum from a large paint bucket. She kept rhythm with most songs. The bucket was decorated with plastic beads and crow feathers. The drum was difficult to keep in tune, but the accomplishment made her smile.

Annabelle gave the drum to her younger sister, along with a large portion of our furniture and clothing. She says material goods are a hindrance to human progression.

5

The sky outside the bus remains dark with sections of gray clouds and the light of stars. Annabelle leans her head against the glass. She coughs lightly as she speaks.

"Remember the scented t-shirts you tried to make?"

"This isn't like that."

"Did anyone see your feet?"

"It's too dark."

She laughs again and closes her eyes. The air conditioning unit is above us and positioned directly towards my head. Annabelle uses a sweater to protect her knees from the cold air. I consider using the bathroom.

I notice Annabelle beginning to sleep. Her legs twitch and she repositions herself several times. I recline my chair and stretch both legs beneath the seat in front of me. I stare at the ceiling and concentrate on the vibration of the air conditioner.

6

We wake up several times during the night from continuous stops and refueling. I notice a different driver as our bus enters Texas. He is a large man, possibly in his early thirties. The man attempts to smoke cigarettes with his window slightly open. The scent of tobacco circulates through the interior of the bus. Annabelle wakes up long enough to notice.

She pulls the sweater over her face and returns to sleep. I sing to her, watching vehicles on the highway as they pass. The driver throws a cigarette out the window. He coughs and sits straight in the seat. The bus is silent again. Most passengers are asleep. I close my eyes and lean against Annabelle's shoulder. The scent of vodka on her clothing comforts me and helps me sleep.

7

We have an early breakfast at a station in Flatonia, Texas. We eat cinnamon rolls from a vending machine and share an orange juice from a souvenir shop. Annabelle buys an ashtray in the shape of Texas. I use the bathroom and lay down on a wooden bench.

"I wish we had something to put in this juice."

"Too early for me."

"You've done it before."

"Not right now."

"We don't have a bottle, anyway."

"Maybe in Houston. We have to switch buses there."

"You have the plane tickets right?"

"They're in my backpack under the bus."

"What time does the flight leave?"

"We'll be in Miami for awhile. I'm glad you brought those books."

"You can play guitar there."

"Maybe."

"Remember when you played guitar on Stone Avenue and that guy came up and started complaining?"

Our bus number is called and we board with the others. I notice the couple previously seated in front of us remain at the station in Flatonia. Annabelle asks if I want the window seat. I decline and she sits down. Most passengers are sleeping as the bus pulls away. There is a new bus driver. He is a young man with thick glasses drinking from a two-liter bottle of cola. I finish my cinnamon roll and rest my head on Annabelle's shoulder. We quickly fall asleep as the bus moves towards our destination. The sun begins to rise and the stars fade into the clouds. No one talks or complains.

8

We arrive at the Houston terminal late in the afternoon. The air in the bus is dry and there is a general discomfort among the passengers. The bus pulls into the station and the driver announces the transfer numbers for the main lines. Annabelle massages her back with both hands as I collect her suitcase and gather the books. I place an empty bag of potato chips into the seat cushion. Annabelle speaks loudly.

"Did you see anywhere that sells liquor?"

"I forgot to look."

"Maybe that little store over there."

"What store?"

"It's behind the other bus."

"I don't know."

"I thought you said we'd be here by early morning, it's almost three now."

"You're the one who said that."

"My back aches from these seats."

"Why don't you try one of those meditation techniques in that book?"

"I have been, but it's hard to do it by yourself."

"The book you gave me said that there is no male or female, only a single Karmic stream."

Annabelle rolls her eyes and we proceed down the aisle. The crowd moves quickly as they gather their belongings. My feet stick to the floor as we walk. I can feel the air from the exit door. It is a calm and sensual breeze that filters through the dry atmosphere of the bus. I am in need of a bathroom.

We stand outside the Houston terminal as the station employees sort through luggage under the bus. I am handed a large backpack after my name is called. Annabelle immediately searches for our plane tickets. She smiles and places the envelope in her suitcase.

"Did you finish that song, David?"

"Which one?"

"The one about the ocean?"

"Finished a few days ago."

"I think you should play that one for the tourist board."

"Maybe."

9

Annabelle receives all of her baggage and sits down with my backpack on the sidewalk. I wait patiently for my guitar. The men hurry to unload, tossing bags to their owners. A man secures one section of the compartment doors and empties out the remainder of the storage area. He removes a large suitcase and then my guitar. I hold the case with two hands. The fabric is damaged and torn.

I glance at Annabelle as she stumbles over to the bus. We stand silently for a moment before she speaks.

"Excuse me, sir?"

"Yes."

"What is this?"

"That's how it looked when I pulled it out."

The young man searches through the empty compartments as we watch. He motions his shoulders in a disbelieving gesture. I recognize his sympathy. He tells me he is sorry and directs us to the customer service counter inside the terminal.

I pause outside the door to inspect the damage. My guitar is partially cracked through the center. The neck is bent and there are thin pieces of wood along the interior of the case. The guitar is functional but difficult to tune.

Annabelle holds on to my waist as we walk into the bus station with our luggage. The employee's directions are vague, but we are first in line at the customer service counter.

I tell the woman my situation and explain to her how important the guitar is. She instructs me to fill out a *Mishandled Baggage Form* and to leave an address and phone number where I can be reached.

"Well, our bus to Miami leaves in less than an hour, do you have any type of insurance for something like this?"

"I'm not sure."

"And from Miami we'll be on a plane and we don't have a permanent address where we're going."

"You can contact us at the number on the form after your flight lands and give us your information, but you'll need this *MBF* number to process the request. You should probably put some shoes on too."

"My guitar was destroyed by your bus."

"After I handle your request I can examine the situation, but it's unusual to establish the cause of a problem like yours. It could have been broken before you got on the bus."

Annabelle sits down on the bench behind me. She looks tired and uneasy. I finish the paperwork and explain again to the woman how essential the guitar is. I give her details on the amount of furniture and appliances we gave away. She resumes her professional composure and I exit the line. The man and the young boy that were behind us on the bus are in line. They appear frustrated. The boy carries the flashlight and a small plastic bag full of clothing. The man stands proud in his patches.

Annabelle notices my disgust and begins to rub my leg while I sit beside her on the bench. Her eyes show compassion and her smile has a slight posture of guilt.

"What are we going to do now?"

"What do you mean?"

"I can't perform with this guitar."

"Why not?"

"Because."

"Maybe we can fix it."

"They should buy me a new one."

"Did you see the size of the suitcase that was on top of it?"

"Not really."

"Come on, let's get a bottle."

"To celebrate?"

"Do you want to be in Tucson for the rest of your life?"

"Not really."

"Well, let's go. We can't refund the plane tickets anyway."

"The tourist board won't take me with a guitar like this."

Annabelle is silent. She reaches in her suitcase for a book. She hands me the copy of *Mahayana Massage and Yoga Consciousness*. The book is a thick, hardbound edition with pictures and lengthy advice on the perception of the Self through intensive massage and meditation. I page through the book, looking briefly at the photographs and charts. Annabelle smiles continuously. I read a small section of the first chapter before returning the book to her.

"What does this have to do with anything?"

"Guess."

"I don't know."

"Guess."

"I don't know."

"When we get to St. Martin, I can call the French temple."

"And?"

"I can offer these services to members of the community who are interested in spiritual development. Therapeutic massage is gaining popularity down there. It's an untapped market. And with those classes I took over the summer and the diagrams in this book, I can charge a small fee to the public and we can work things from there. Maybe buy a new guitar."

"I don't know."

"It's a good idea."

"Do we have money left in the account?"

"Let's get a bottle across the street."

"Don't you think we should talk about the whole thing?"

"It's a good idea."

Annabelle stands up from the bench. She repositions her backpack and motions me to stand. I agree and she directs me out of the terminal towards the store across the street. No one in the station notices us as we walk past. We all have similar opportunities and aspirations for the future.

The air outside the station is warm and floats over us with a passionate touch. Annabelle pulls on my arm as she reads the front sign of the store. It is a small liquor outlet with large neon signs on the front. Its door is open. We pause before we cross the intersection. Annabelle begins to lightly massage my shoulders and twist my earlobes with her fingers. We embrace each other on the sidewalk. The hug is awkward due to the heavy weight of our luggage. We walk toward the liquor store. The intersection is busy. My bare feet slide gracefully across the asphalt.

Ninety Percent

"We are individuals of circumstance. No one is wrong and no one is right. We are the recipients of a predetermined injustice. We must overcome."- **Hal Patterson: Martinsville, Virginia 1983**

1

The neighborhoods were filled with celebration and relief. Hal's supporters assembled in an improvised parade down Church Street. The procession was led by five police cars. The election was a success.

Hal's opponent was the city treasurer, Dan Irwin. He wore thick glasses and fashioned himself in suits and ties. Dan is a sixty-year-old man and a member of the Republican Party. He showed little acceptance of Hal. He is a retired officer of the county sheriff's department. Dan's proposals included simple budget solutions and city tax exemptions. Dan was uninspiring.

Hal's campaign was popularized by a group of friends who volunteered to attach election posters on telephone poles throughout the city. Hal placed a number of advertisements in the singles section of the newspaper. He would date the respondents frequently. The percentage of female voters was the highest in state history for an independent political party.

Hal was raised in Axton, outside Martinsville. His presence was well known in the community from his assistance with Red Cross blood donations at the YMCA. Much of his past has been correlated with his rise to municipal power.

Hal graduated from Averett College with a degree in business marketing. A year before the election, he held weekly dinners for the homeless on the corner of Market and Broad Street. He bought and prepared the food himself. Hal convinced nearly two hundred members of the community to register to vote. He was built with the understanding of social progression.

"We each use the acquired knowledge in our lives for different reasons. I have examined our situation and choose to implement my past experiences with the present conditions in which we preside."

2

Hal was a thin man, forty-three years old when his self-designed kingdom began to collapse. Throughout his term, he dressed himself in blue jeans and golf shirts. His physical image was not a concern. His appearance seemed standard for the level of control he needed. Hal drove a gray mini van to all public events.

3

The first official decision Hal made after the election was to foreclose on unused property in the West section of the city. Demolition crews quickly destroyed all buildings within a three-acre area. A horticultural team prepared the soil.

The property now includes several varieties of apple and pear trees. Seventeen rows of grape vines cover the front section of the farm. Root vegetables and other seasonal crops are planted annually throughout the compound. The city has recently purchased the adjacent lot for an expansion next year.

The plantation covers a large section of land. The majority of labor is provided through community service workers and elderly volunteers. The land supplies Martinsville twice a year. Hal's greenhouse diagrams are being studied and slightly adjusted to correspond with the larger area. It is a continuous project.

Hal was able to see the community receive products on one occasion. The first year after sowing and transplanting, the tomato plants and pumpkin vines did well. Consumers were able to save nearly half the cost of store prices. A large section of the harvest was donated to regional shelters and charities. Hal spoke at the ribbon cutting ceremony.

"Life began in the garden. We must establish a tradition of togetherness and a pattern of shared interests. We need to realize the importance of nature and the beautiful way the earth provides. We need to practice the imitation."

4

The corresponding economic decline for the local agricultural trade was an unexpected result. Family farms began to lose profit. Migrant workers lost jobs. The unemployment rate increased five percent over a two week period following the first harvest. Hal took immediate action.

The town's migrant workers were offered any available positions from the city. Others found work in local furniture production or the textile industry. Hal and his assistants developed an organization to assist the farms in generating a larger distribution along the East coast. He offered the agricultural community a portion of the city's recreation budget to help finance the cost of machinery for advanced production.

5

Hal guaranteed in his inaugural speech, a lower crime rate in Martinsville. During the reign of the previous mayor, criminal activity was at its highest in the town's history. This was partially due to the lack of political enforcement and the inability to maintain social control over minorities. Hal advised the newspaper to begin a daily police report to document the improvements. He enjoyed the publicity. Hal seemed fearless and certain. He smiled with encouragement. The accident at the Speedway was a tragic loss for Martinsville.

6

Under Hal's direction, the city ordered an additional supply of vehicles for the police department. Five of the cars were equipped with dark tint on each window. The headlights were connected to a regulator that would activate every five hours for three minutes. The vehicles were placed in select areas of town, with no officers inside. The position of the cars changed daily. Few people knew about the experiment.

Over the year, criminal activity decreased considerably in each area where the vehicles were stationed. The budget for police labor remained the same. The citizens were pleased. Hal spoke to a large crowd outside the courthouse shortly before the end of his career.

"Life is not what you do, it's how you make it look on the outside. Our entire existence is based on a principle of ninety percent presentation, ten percent actualization. A book will forever be judged by its cover. We need to realize the importance of the disguise that covers our surroundings, and revel in its correlation with the human soul."

Hal's communication skills were the background of his success. No one could explain how the police force suddenly expanded while net earnings appeared unaffected. Citizens began to question Hal and his unconventional methods. Most assumed that local taxes would fund the remainder of police wages.

Hal assured that no taxations would be necessary under the new economic plan. He spoke with a promising smile. Rumors began to circulate that the agricultural firms were losing too much money.

"The goals of our community are extensive. In order to push ourselves forward we must pull ourselves back. For every pull there is always a push. The monetary value of such circumstance is an indirect consequence of perseverance."

7

After lengthy criticism regarding traffic problems were filed in the city's *Neighborhood Complaint Boxes*, Hal and his municipal supremacy developed a quick solution.

Hal approved an adjustment to traffic signal timing. Yellow lights were lengthened to six seconds along the main road and remained at four seconds at the smaller intersections. Hal's approach incorporated a geometrical pattern based on the average speed of a domestic automobile. The longer amount of time it required a driver to make the light, the less congestion would occur on the streets. The system was developed and maintained by a company from Richmond.

In defense of his decision to hire an outside corporation, Hal explained that he was able to access funds from the state to finance the changes. He confirmed that local taxes would not be affected. Hal stood motionless. The public was deeply in love.

"No one person can acknowledge themselves as a superior being. Every creature is a portion of the whole. Why shadow yourselves with doubt and frustration? Become your own individual and progress in your own direction."

In a similar effort to handle the traffic situation, Hal employed juvenile offenders from Henry County. The juveniles were instructed to locate bicycles from around the city limits. The bicycles were then rebuilt by a team of city-employed laborers and then painted a bright green. The bikes were placed everywhere around Martinsville. Anyone could travel to their destination and easily find another bicycle to take home.

The children would avoid all punishment relating to their offense if they complied with Hal's policies. They accepted Hal's proposal with confidence. The children trusted Hal.

Few people were aware of the actual situation. Hal explained the necessity of the system in a televised broadcast. He spoke with an animated voice.

"The incorporation of environment-friendly travel is essential to the future of our existence. We will all benefit from this service. Think of it as a gift to Martinsville. The Blue Ridge will be forever thankful under a clean, blue sky."

It was a cooperative system of transportation. Much of Hal's operation had been experimental. Hal had the courage and skill to proceed.

The juveniles appointed to the patrol, quickly found that participating in crime was similar to a standard occupation. They became uninterested in illegal trade. This helped to further minimize criminal activity and also assisted in decreasing traffic and air pollution in the downtown area. Hal was delighted. He began to smoke cigarettes and attend evening church services at the Presbyterian Church on Patrick Henry Street.

8

The local agriculture industry was experiencing continuous financial difficulty. A downsizing of staff was necessary to stay competitive with the East coast corporations. A movement was quickly organized to confront Hal and his methods of progression.

9

The sheriff's department combined forces with the management of *Virginia Produce* and *Southern VA Farms*. They became powerful allies. Dan Irwin was known for his connections inside the sheriff's department. He was also involved in the movement. Dan was a closet outlaw.

Three months following Hal's decision to recalculate the traffic lights, the agricultural operative began their first physical resistance. The sheriff's department was instructed to arrest or fine Martinsville citizens whenever possible.

The yellow lights soon began to restrict traffic, causing numerous speed violations and miscellaneous accidents. The incentive for vehicles to accelerate at yellow lights began to have negative results for drivers.

This caused the crime rate to increase significantly. The newspaper began to print their police log on the front page. Dan Irwin held a resistant grin. The local farms continued to suffer financially.

Hal's dating advertisements became public knowledge. The newspaper presented a half page article about Hal and his romantic endeavors. Two women interviewed claimed that Hal had attempted to control their vote. Hal denied all accusations.

"In no such manner have I ever disrespected my position with Martinsville. I value our citizens and our town. I am here to govern and to assist. I have never taken advantage of my situation."

As the opposition strengthened, Hal focused his career on secondary matters to improve status with the town. He made an unauthorized decision to construct asphalt swimming pools in low rent areas of Martinsville and the surrounding county. He was in the newspaper each day during the construction. The publicity was damaging to Hal's self-esteem. The reporters were enjoying themselves.

Hal refused to attend any of the grand openings. He was informed about the agricultural conspiracy. Hal was not afraid. He was cautious and prepared.

Hal remained active in certain community events and he volunteered much of his time to the YMCA. He taught an English language course on weekend afternoons. Hal frequently attended races at the Martinsville Speedway. Hal was a figure of sincerity. He received threatening telephone messages daily.

Hal relocated from his home on Waller Road to a friend's house downtown. He needed to reorganize himself for the conflict. He needed to reclaim the system he had created.

10

The city police began to encounter negative influences from both sides of the struggle. The sheriff's department had connections in police management. Hal controlled a large section of their budget. Martinsville was powerless. Hal and his aggressors became competitive. Each side desired personal triumph.

Hal arranged a brief solution to the problem. It was an opportunity for individuals from various political backgrounds to associate freely and unobstructed. He invented a holiday. Hal designated the day: *Irreverence Day*. The celebration represented the trial and error of community development.

11

Hal apologized to local farm owners and offered tax exclusions and financial reimbursements. He publicly accepted his failures and declared an abolishment to inequality. He exposed the involvement of Dan Erwin and the sheriff's department, revealing clerical documents in connection with their arrest strategies. Hal was televised on both local channels.

"In history, we have attempted to revitalize the community with new ideas. Change is a difficult concept for many of us. It is a costume. There can be no revisions without patience and endurance. We need to hold onto what we have. We need to do our part in making Martinsville and Henry County a better place to live."

Hal spoke with encouragement. The day was uncomfortable and cold. Hal announced that local government offices should close immediately. He released a tentative schedule of events for the evening.

12

Hal made arrangements with a local grocery distributor to provide the city with a variety of picnic food and beverages. The citizens were happy. Hal was pleased.

The festivities symbolized the need for improvement. Hal attended the celebration dressed in a collared shirt and brown corduroys. His blonde hair was respectable and neatly combed. Hal made his appearance with a young woman who works in the tax department. She complemented Hal's disposition and added strength to his morale. They were together throughout the evening.

After a lengthy speech, which integrated members of city government into the holiday celebration, Hal escorted his guest to a small restaurant where a young man with an acoustic guitar was singing traditional folk songs. Hal sat in a chair beside the young woman. The songs acknowledged freedom and chronicled the life of labor workers in the Blue Ridge Mountains. A woman began to play violin. Hal stood and applauded the performers. He lit a cigarette and waved his hands at the audience. The situation was perfect. Hal was in control. He sat down and crossed his legs.

13

Late in the evening, Hal was approached by a representative of the Martinsville Speedway. The man stood much taller than Hal and articulated himself with heavy facial movements. He invited Hal to compete in a celebrity race the following week at the Speedway. Hal declined with an overwhelming sigh. The man explained to Hal that a large percentage of the revenue would be donated to the Children's Fund of Southern Virginia.

Hal made a quick gesture to his female friend. She smiled. Hal accepted the challenge. He enjoyed the simplicity of the sport and regularly watched the events on television. Hal would compete in a car sponsored by a local supermarket. Martinsville would be proud. Dan Irwin was forgotten. The sheriff's department kept quiet.

14

Irreverence Day was celebrated again this year. The event was well planned and skillfully designed as a method to demonstrate the power of municipal awareness.

The Speedway functioned as a facility for the events. The track was decorated with red and black ribbon. The Speedway administration dedicated a portion of the seating in Hal's memory. The city was able to fund a professional jazz ensemble and an assortment of children's activities. The celebrations helped Martinsville citizens to realize the significance of their government and its relationship to their lives.

Martinsville residents have become comfortable with structured opinions and rationed law. Following the accident at the Speedway, Hal's commitment to the city was further understood and appreciated. The Mayor Pro Tem accepted Hal's position with admiration. He was chosen during Hal's term. He is a highly regarded member of city council.

Hal's ideas linger through the local government. His intelligence has been recycled and implemented with various outcomes. Hal's accident was a tragic loss.

15

The community takes advantage of the low cost produce. Most of the smaller farms have sold their land and relocated further south. The mayor has improved on many of Hal's earlier projects. There has been a political recovery in Henry County. Large industries are negotiating land contracts with the city. Martinsville has been reborn. There are two harvests each year and the local economy is beginning to expand. The County is proposing a new elementary school near the river. The crime rate is down.

16

Hal was buried in a small cemetery in Axton, next to his mother. The ceremony was performed by a Presbyterian minister. Five police cars escorted the funeral procession. A large group of supporters and friends attended the services.

Hal's methods of control quickly integrated themselves into daily life in Southern Virginia. His simple and extraordinary ideas changed how Martinsville lives. The dating section in the newspaper is larger than the police log. Romance is everywhere. Citizens ride bicycles to work.

Thank you, Hal. It was a good year.

X is for Xylophone

*"What good mothers and fathers instinctively feel like doing for their babies is usually best after all." - **Dr. Benjamin Spock***

1

The cold air of the evening circulates through each room of the house. Christopher is in the kitchen training for the tournament. He occasionally shouts and falls to the mat. The window in the living room is open. Our home is hidden from the main road by a thick section of trees. I amuse myself with Angela's hair as she begins to fall asleep. The radio is broadcasting a compilation of philharmonic orchestras.

Angela and I lay on the couch with a poetry book. She enjoys the pictures and the complexity of rhyme. Christopher borrowed the book from the library last week. It is a wire bound publication of traditional Romanian verse. The book is illustrated with artwork from 19th century European painters. The images are colorful and intricately detailed. The poems have been translated by a couple living in England. Angela likes the wolf drawing on the book's cover. She laughs and points to the background, demanding an explanation for the absurdity of the creature. I explain with a lengthy story from my childhood. She falls to sleep with the book held in both arms.

Christopher wears a white towel around his neck as he enters the room. His clothing is layered with sweat stains and he appears concerned about something. He sits on the couch next to my feet. The fabric of his athletic clothing makes an uncomfortable noise. Christopher removes the book from Angela's hands.

"I wanted to talk to her before she went to bed."

"She fell asleep when we were reading."

"Did she like it?"

"She liked the paintings."

"I found a picture book about the history of China. The photographs are great."

"You can read it tomorrow."

Christopher is a martial arts instructor, concentrating on the Northern Shaolin style of Kung Fu. His students are traveling to Tampa for the State Championships. He has been training them everyday for the past two months. The win could bring his school national attention.

2

The cultivation of Angela's intellect has been his project for the past four years. I agree with most of the conditions he has created. Her progression is natural. Her ambition seems limitless.

Angela is a beautiful child with straight blonde hair and light skin. Her eyes are an intimate green. Christopher has begun a training program that keeps Angela active around the house. He keeps a record of her achievements on a chalkboard in the hallway.

Her diet consists of raw fruit and vegetables, chewable vitamins, and baked bread. She does not know the taste of other foods. Christopher and I share similar eating habits, although Christopher has an affection for chewing gum.

3

"After the tournament, we should start working on her motor skills again, try to develop a structured routine."

"Think she's ready for that?"

"We won't know. She could be the greatest Shaolin in America."

"I think she might be getting bored."

"What?"

"She needs more stimulation."

"I thought we agreed on a dog?"

"That might work."

"We've gone over this four years now, Pam."

Angela turns over and mumbles in her sleep. She caresses the couch cushion. Her legs remain still. Christopher becomes frustrated and carries Angela to her bedroom. He returns to the kitchen, sets his equipment aside and portions himself a bowl of fresh cucumbers. He sits down at the kitchen table by himself. He eats with bamboo chopsticks. Christopher closes his eyes as he chews.

"I'm going to lay down in bed. Do you want to come in after you finish eating?"

"Sure."

"I'll see you in a minute."

"Sure."

Christopher remains in the kitchen long after I fall asleep.

4

Angela wakes up early. She runs into our bedroom with a knitted blanket. She plays with my hair and sits on my chest. Christopher rolls himself to the far side of the bed. I take Angela firmly under her arms and we move to the living room. The poetry book is on the floor.

"Can we read the book again?"

"Not right now. We need breakfast."

"Grapes, grapes, grapes!"

"And strawberries."

"Juice!"

Angela runs into the kitchen before me. She finds the strawberries in the refrigerator. Christopher wakes up in the excitement. He scuffles awkwardly out the bedroom door wearing nothing. His chest hair is fully exposed. Christopher believes the common image of the nude body will relieve sexual tension during adolescence.

"Good morning."

"Daddy!"

"What are you doing up so early?"

"Grapes!"

"Grapes are good. Do we have any bread in the fridge?"

Christopher looks at me curiously. It is difficult to avoid eye contact with his penis. He stands naked in the kitchen. I wash strawberries in the sink. He does not realize how unusual it is.

"I don't work until the afternoon."

"Want a strawberry?"

"Let me look in the fridge first."

"Daddy, can we read the wolf book?"

"Wolf?"

"She's talking about the book in the living room."

"We can read after we practice our exercises."

"Exercise!"

5

Angela's untainted emotions and her lack of knowledge about the world provide little accuracy to Christopher's diagram. Before her birth, he wrote a fifteen-page theory on the ideal stages of childhood development. His main point is the suppression of social contact. Christopher believes that to properly raise a child is to protect her from an artificial existence while she is young and vulnerable. I agree in some aspects. His constant affirmations have become difficult to understand. I have not read an entire newspaper in four years.

The process began while I was pregnant. Christopher and I agreed to tell no one about the situation. As my weight increased, I was confined to the house until the day of delivery. Christopher gave our television to the neighbor. He painted the bathroom with a tiny sponge. We hired a mid-wife.

Our families live in upstate New York, far from the Gulf coast. We have kept minimal contact with family members. Angela has been the center of our lives. She has become a project. It is part of the hypothesis.

6

"Ok, Angela. Now take the big part of your hand."

"Big hand!"

"Yes."

"Hand."

"And point it like this."

"My hand is big."

"Yes, like this."

Christopher has dressed himself in sweat pants and a baseball hat. His wrist is slightly bent and his fingertips are set above her eyes. His hairline is hidden under the hat.

Angela laughs, then claps her hands and kicks at the air. I watch her closely as I clean the kitchen table with a wet cloth.

"Your left foot set like this and your other foot back here."

Angela stands in a similar position. She laughs again and kicks the air. Christopher stands straight with his back against the wall. Angela stomps her feet on the hardwood floor. I continue to clean.

"Take your hand and turn it."

"This?"

Christopher holds her hand. She pulls away and begins to spin around with the heels of her feet. Angela runs wildly through the living room and returns with a book. She sits on the floor and turns through the pages. Christopher becomes anxious.

"The wolf!"

"We can read it later. We need to finish our exercises."

"1,2,3,4."

Angela's behavior and attentiveness have weakened over the past year. She has difficulty concentrating on a single issue. She often forgets to use the toilet. Christopher sees no reason for concern. He says that Angela is behaving in a perfectly unsociable manner. He claims that she is acting on instinct and not through a conditioned response. He is proud of her failures and arrogant of her accomplishments.

"Christopher, just let her look at the book."

"All she knows is books and food, Pam."

"She knows more than that."

"Not what she needs to."

"Needs?"

"Like honor and strength."

"She has no sense of those words."

"There is no sense."

Christopher returns to the bedroom. He whispers something to himself as he opens the door. Angela holds the book in her hands. She turns the pages quickly, moving her head in a repeating pattern with each page. She stops at the last picture and shuts the book.

Angela walks happily into the kitchen. She sits on a small stool near the telephone. She imitates the radio announcer as the music begins. Christopher falls asleep in his sweatpants with the bedroom door open.

7

Angela stands on the stool and begins to dance. Her hips sway easily and her hands vibrate. It is a physical response to the rhythm. She jumps down to the floor. I finish cleaning the table and turn the radio volume down. The scene has returned to its usual state.

I suggest a game of cards. Angela becomes stubborn. She insists on going in the backyard. I suggest water paints. She smiles and scratches her stomach. Angela looks for the keys to unlock the backdoor. She walks out of the kitchen.

As I wipe the cabinet doors, I hear the rattle of keys. Angela runs into the room with a small soccer ball. She hands me a set of keys. We walk quietly towards the backdoor. The handle is difficult to turn. The sun is set high above the horizon. The fresh air is an instant relief.

Angela does not have many toys. The soccer ball and a container of sand with twigs and stones are the only playthings in the yard. The grass is uncut and the trees are spread throughout the lawn. Our house is surrounded by forest. We have few neighbors and friends rarely visit.

Angela kicks the ball and runs after it. She points at birds and squirrels. The animals appear to give her a sense of the bigger world. She laughs.

"Bird."

"Can you hear him sing?"

"Two birds."

"Kick the ball over here."

"Ok."

Angela steps back and releases a mighty kick. The ball rolls past me under the steps. Angela motions her arms in an imitation of self-defense. She laughs and runs to the sand and begins to dig. She throws a rock across the yard. She buries the remaining stones in the sand. I reach for the soccer ball.

"Pass it back to me."

"Ok."

She kicks the ball with extreme force. She screams violently. I stop the ball with my feet and toss it back under the stairs. Angela continues to dig and bury. I reach for the keys in my pocket.

"Angela, let's go."

"Ok."

Christopher sleeps in the bedroom. A squirrel runs quickly across the yard, bouncing itself onto a tree. The car is sealed behind a garage door. Angela walks toward me, her shirt covered with sand and a smile pasted across her face.